The Elephant Heist

Rucha Dixit

SRL PUBLISHING

The Elephant Heist

Rucha Dixit

B. PUBLISHING

SRL Publishing Ltd
London
www.srlpublishing.co.uk

First published worldwide by SRL Publishing in 2023

ISBN: 978-19150732-1-1

1 3 5 7 9 10 8 6 4 2

A CIP catalogue record for this book is available from the
British Library

SRL Publishing is a Climate Positive publisher offsetting more
carbon emissions than it emits.

*For my children, Pratham, and Siya — my staunchest
critics and biggest believers*

Glossary

Appa – Form of address for father.

Bajrang Bali – God of strength and power also known as Hanuman.

Bidi – a type of cheap cigarette made of unprocessed tobacco wrapped in leaves.

Bheesti – Water carrier.

Chowkidar – watchman.

Damru – A two-headed drum, typically made of wood with leather drum heads at both ends.

Dhaal – lentil soup.

Dhoti – a garment worn by male Hindus, consisting of a piece of material tied around the waist and extending to cover most of the legs.

Diya – small earthen lamp that holds a wick soaked in oil/ghee.

Dost – Friend.

Ganji – a vest.

Ghee – clarified butter.

Haldi – turmeric.

Hanuman – Another name for Bajrang Bali, the god of strength and power.

Howdah – A seat for riding on the back of an elephant.

Jalebee – fried chickpea batter dipped in saffron flavoured sugar syrup.

Jamun – Java plum.

Janwar – beast.

Kajal – a black paste used in India as a cosmetic around the eyes.

Khansama: Cook.

Khitmagar – bearer/butler of a household.

Koonki – A specially trained elephant used to hunt wild elephants.

Kumkum – red powder used by Hindus on deities. Also used by Hindu women to mark a red spot on the forehead.

Langoor – monkey.

Mahout – Elephant trainer.

Sahib – A polite title for a man / Sir.

Shikar - Hunting as a sport.

Shiva - Indian God.

Shukriya – Thank you.

Chapter One

Once upon a time, around a hundred years ago, in the land of elephants and spices, lived a boy who had a storm in his chest and a twinkle in his eye. It was a time when India was under Crown Rule: the time of The British Raj.

The boy was Indian; his skin the colour of earth, his eyes and hair as black as night. Most of him was dark and brown and black on the exterior and within him flickered a zest for life – an unpolished diamond, he was. And thus his name was Heera – which means *diamond* in Hindi.

Heera was the son of Vasu, an Indian tribal woman who used to collect wood in the forest. On one of her routine wood-collecting expeditions, she had given birth to Heera. That day, she had walked out of the forest as casually as she would on any other day, except she held a baby to her bosom, instead of a bundle of wood on her head.

Born in the wilderness – under the cloudless, blue Indian sky and amongst the bird song – Heera had a piece of the forest etched within him. By the time he was seven years old, he could climb most trees with the swiftness of a squirrel and could swing on branches with the agility of a monkey. Snakes fascinated him more than they scared common people, and he could tell which ones were venomous, just by looking. He knew most medicinal herbs there were to know and where to find them. Wild fruits such as wood apples, java plums, gooseberries, custard apples, coconuts, and bananas were his staple diet. And he always had a glut of these, eagerly supplied to him by Bali – a magnificent, eight-foot-tall elephant.

Heera and Vasu lived in a small hut at the edge of the forest. Thatched with bamboo and hay, the hut's roof slanted at a precarious angle to the walls which were plastered with soil and cow dung. Heera had painted these naturally ochre walls with a mixture of rice paste, water, and gum, using a chewed bamboo stick as a paintbrush. The inside of the hut smelled of wood, smoke, ash, earth, animal dung, and sweat. And the only thing that glinted in the hut, with whatever light it could catch, was a piece of a broken mirror that had been embedded in the mud wall by an insistent Heera and his reluctant mother.

"No, no. We can't be keeping this." Vasu had looked at the mirror with disgust as if it were a dead rat. "Where did you find it?"

"Under a tree." Heera, then only five, had pointed outside the hut, dejection strewn across his face like the dust that coated it from all the digging he had done to discover the mirror buried under the ground.

"Someone might have buried it there. Nobody keeps broken mirrors inside their homes. It's a bad omen, child." Vasu rubbed at his grubby face with the loose end of her saree.

Heera's guileless black eyes batted and grew as wide as plates, with wonder, as he turned the mirror in his hands. "Look how beautiful." The mirror – an irregular pentagon – winked in the sunlight through the window. "It's my treasure, Ma. Please let me keep it," he implored.

Vasu's insides warmed with affection. She couldn't get herself to say no. The worse omen could only be an unhappy child. *Her* unhappy child.

It all started with a loud BANG that set off a cacophony of birds ringing through the forest one afternoon. Heera was in his hut, painting diamond shapes on the walls that looked unbearably naked to him after his mother had given them a fresh coat of cow dung a few days back. The paintings, even though plain white, added colour to his life.

Heera was busy admiring the half-done wall and was wondering what patterns to draw around the irregular piece of mirror, to accentuate it.

Spitting into the palms of both hands, he slid them through his longish hair, looking into the piece of mirror as he did so. He repeated this a couple of times until all his shoulder-length tresses had been slicked back and set. *I'm never losing these, even if Ma doesn't like them.*

Satisfied, he picked up an apple and sank his teeth into the crisp sweetness.

The gun shot shook him. The mirror on the wall trembled. The apple fell to the floor and tumbled away. Heera's stomach bunched up to his throat.

It had to be the *Sahibs* hunting.

The first time Heera had heard a gunshot was a few years ago. Then, he didn't know what he had heard. Like any curious child, he asked his mother. Vasu had tried her best to avoid answering him. She couldn't bear to burden his innocent mind with the cruelty of the world. However, Heera, who was as obstinate as a mule, didn't give up and Vasu had to speak up.

"Must be the sahibs on *shikar*," Vasu had said reluctantly.

4

That answer didn't satisfy Heera's appetite.

Who were these sahibs?

What was shikar?

He dug at Vasu until he tired her. And although he had got the truth out of her, he had found it hard to comprehend. Why and how could someone kill for fun? Whose vile and preposterous idea was that?

The thought of the atrocity lingered in his juvenile mind even though he dodged it for days and pushed it aside when it pained him. Finally, he buried it in a dark corner of his mind.

A few months later, he had found young Bali, struggling to get out of a deep mud pit flooded with the monsoon rains. Falling in love with Bali changed things – for the worse. He loved him like his child, his best friend, his brother, his everything. It was like letting a piece of himself walk outside him. Love made him vulnerable. It excavated that dark corner in his mind and let out his nastiest fears. What if it was Bali next?

Heera's heart sank when the gun went off. And what followed next left him in a state of shock and panic that rose and rose in him until it had him in its grasp, paralysed from head to toe.

It was a sharp, high-pitched trumpet that cut through the forest. And Heera recognised it. Were his fears coming to life? He couldn't breathe. This wasn't a playful, happy trumpet. It was a cry of fury and pain.

BALI!!! No. No. No. Please God. NO.

His soul contorted with anguish. Forcing himself out of the terror that overpowered his mind and body, he ran in the direction of the sound, legs flying.

Another trumpet followed.

Bali. I'm coming, dost. I'm coming.

Heera ran unthinking and unstoppable, channelling all his fear into his legs, his heart thrashing against his ribcage. He knew the forest well and threw himself over the branches and ducked under them as he ran. Wind whipped through his long tresses, sending wisps of hair flying in tangles. The trumpeting continued, helping to direct him. Thorns and branches bruised and cut his skin as he lanced through the dense undergrowth. But it didn't matter. Nothing mattered more than Bali. Heera's limber body vaulted over puddles of water left behind by the monsoon and skidded through sludge, sometimes falling. Nevertheless, he got up and ran. His legs smarted with exhaustion, but his spirit would not quit.

After a while, in the distance, he could see a clearing in the forest. He saw some men on foot and a mahout riding an elephant, surrounding what looked like the head of an elephant on the ground.

The men were shouting in a mix of excitement and exasperation.

Heera by now was covered head to toe with a thick paste of mud; face included. Not even Vasu would have recognised him, unless she looked very closely. He ran as far as he could go without being seen and hid behind a tree. He then pulled himself up on to a branch to gain a vantage point.

An elephant's head was bobbing in and out of a ditch on the ground below. A koonki stood above and the mahout on his neck was throwing a rope down into the ditch trying to lasso the elephant. It was an agonising sight in itself but, within a second, what Heera noticed made the agony excruciating – the conspicuous pink-beige triangular patch of skin on the forehead of the trapped elephant. Terror tore through every inch of his body with the realisation it was Bali! Tears blurred his vision. An overpowering sense of helplessness choked him.

"BALI!" Heera screamed with all his might. His voice drowned in the commotion of the shouting men and the trumpeting elephants.

Another elephant appeared, ridden by a mahout on its neck and an English officer on its back, in a howdah. Two shikaris approached and were shouting out to the white man who sat on the elephant. It was hard to tell what they were saying since they were all screaming, their voices colliding with each other. But it looked like they were beckoning him.

"Sahib," Heera muttered to himself, recollecting what Mother had told him. His nostrils flared with raw emotion. Hot indignation exploded within his chest and he set off in the direction of the English officer.

There were far too many to fight. But anger defied logic. He ran as if he had just invented bravery.

The shikaris didn't see him come. Heera launched himself at one of them. The man fell to the ground swearing. Heera showered him with fists. The shikari kicked Heera away and the other seized him and forced him to a standing position by gripping his hair and neck.

"Let him go! Let Bali go," Heera cried, kicking wildly at his captor, tears flooding his face.

"Who are you?" one of the men asked, shaking the boy by his hair. Heera screamed in pain.

"Bali who?" shouted the other.

"That elephant," Heera replied, wiping his tears rapidly, hoping he would be heard, and pointing to Bali. "He's my dost. Don't kill him." Heera looked up at the British officer who sat tall and smug on his elephant as if he owned everyone and everything around him.

The officer glared down at him. His face was all sharp angles. The lines on his forehead looked as if

8

they had deepened with savagery over the years, to look more like trenches. He had a distinctive underbite that gave him the look of a bulldog. His moustache was dense and huge – it took up most of the howdah. And under the thick tuft of the moustache hair sat his lips – the kind that looked as if they hadn't smiled a happy, hearty smile for ages. Although they most certainly had borne the vicious smile, the sadistic smile and the smug smile, amongst many other smiles across all shades of malevolence.

"Oi!" he called to Heera with ridicule, as if he were talking to an insect. "Who the *hell* are you?" he asked, his English words dripping with a heavy British accent.

Heera didn't understand what he said. He simply brought his palms together, from the elbows to the tips of his fingers, in a desperate plea and held them up towards the officer. If grovelling could help save Bali then so be it. His ego was miniscule before the immensity of love that throbbed in his veins for his tusked friend.

"Sahib," he begged. "Don't kill that elephant," he pleaded in Hindi, pointing to Bali and waving his hands in a criss-cross fashion, in front of his chest. "Please let him go."

The officer looked at Bali and then back at Heera. Then he glanced at the men expecting them to translate what the boy had said.

But before they could, Heera spoke in broken English. "E-LAA-FANT-TT," Heera cried in a strong Indian accent with a solid, jarring 'T' sound at the end. His eyes were set on the British officer.

Heera knew a few words in English here and there. Being a smart child, he would gather things around him, even subconsciously, sometimes at the bazaar, or in the main town overhearing school children. He had no friends.

A snort escaped the officer. The shikaris jeered.

"He says, sahib, that let elephant go. Don't kill," one of the men told the officer in English.

The Englishman guffawed. "I don't get *told* what to do, boy. I only *give* orders."

The shikari holding Heera slapped the back of Heera's head.

"Shut up," he scolded. "Don't you dare tell sahib what to do."

"Please, sahib. Please. He's my dost, sahib."

The men roared with laughter and one of them translated Heera's plea for the officer. Heera's eyes moved from the men to the British officer.

"Friend? Huh!" The officer said in English.

Just then Bali shrieked in pain; the trumpet shook the ground. Bali had caught Heera's scent. In his desperation to break free of the noose around his neck, he had gripped the foot of the koonki and tugged at it with all his might. The mahout on top of the koonki had poked Bali with a pointed iron rod.

Heera broke free from the shikari's hold and ran in Bali's direction.

"STOP HIM," bellowed the officer.

The shikari ran after Heera and gripped him by his torso with all his power, lifting him off the ground. Heera kicked his legs in the air frantically. He fought in vain to set himself free from the vice-like grip of the shikari. The officer raised his arm and gestured the shikari to bring Heera to him. The shikari twisted Heera's arms and locked them behind his back, shoving him towards the Englishman.

"Get the hell out of here," shouted the officer. "Else I might blow your *friend's* brains out." He raised his rifle to his eye and took aim at Bali.

Heera flinched. His stomach gnarled with the fear of loss. He dropped to his knees and begged.

"Don't do it. No. NO"

The officer continued, sadistically: "He's a wild beast worthy of being tamed or killed." He shrugged his shoulders. "A fine tusker indeed. Can't make my mind up." He paused, lowering his rifle. "A fine ivory sofa, won't hurt, eh?" He looked at the men below. "Tell him." He raised an eyebrow and nodded. "Tell him what I said."

The men did as they were told and the officer examined the effect of his words on Heera's horrified face, savouring every drop of terror.

Heera could feel his blood boil.

"Some people are worse than animals, sahib. In fact, there are brutes in uniforms, worthy of being tamed," he spat.

The men looked at Heera wide-eyed, then one of them grabbed him by his nape and shook him. "Shut up, you fool," he screamed in Hindi.

The intensity of Heera's insult transcended language. The officer felt it like a blow in the face.

"What did he say?" he yelled at the men.

The men bit their tongues and looked at the ground.

"Can't you hear me? Speak up, you rascals!"

With great reluctance one of them translated Heera's words.

The officer raised an eyebrow – with both surprise and ire – so high, it almost touched his hat. Quick bursts of breath left his flaring nostrils.

"A bit rich coming from a ragamuffin, aye! You've got some nerve," he said, anger pulsing through him. "Come here." He crooked his finger at Heera. His right eye twitched with undiluted hatred while his left one widened its glare over the boy.

The shikari flung Heera towards the officer's elephant. In an instant, the officer slammed the butt of his rifle on Heera's forehead.

Heera staggered backwards, his legs buckling under him. The whole scene span around him before he collapsed to the ground.

"That'll teach you to keep that *insolent* tongue of yours wrapped around your teeth," the officer sneered.

Heera was unconscious before he could hear the words.

Chapter Two

Three years earlier, in the month of June, the Indian monsoon was at its peak. Torrents of rain had thrashed the land, leaving floods in its path. The forest was no exception.

Heera loved the rains as they brought relief from the boiling Indian summer when temperatures soared above forty-five degrees Celsius. And the forest looked greener and prettier and quenched. Monsoon, he thought, was a treat both for the forest and for himself.

He would splash in the water, jump and kick around in the puddles, and swim in the lakes. It was pure bliss. However, his mother always forbade him to get wet. She used to fret about him catching a cold and falling sick. But Heera would do it anyway, without Vasu knowing.

One day, while splashing around, Heera heard a

sharp squeal. Even the sound of the rain, battering against everything that came in its way, wasn't loud enough to hamper the cry. It sounded like an animal in distress, but Heera couldn't tell what animal it could have been. Curious as he was, he couldn't ignore it.

Chasing the sound, he ran through the pouring rain, slipping here and there. And when he got to the place in the heart of the forest where the call was the strongest, he stopped, his heart drumming against his ribs.

Light was poor even in the daytime during the monsoon months. Through the falling rain everything was a blur. All he could see was a sizeable mass of brown and grey squirming and wriggling in distress. Heera slowed down to a walk – every step measured – towards the unknown. Amongst the sounds of the pounding rain and the animal's cries, he could also hear his heart cartwheeling in his chest.

The next few minutes revealed an adolescent elephant, stuck in a mud pit. It had somehow wandered away from its herd and had landed in the pit that was filled with water. The calf had clearly tired itself after numerous attempts to scramble out. It lay helplessly on its side, its desperate cries shrunken to dull whimpers.

Heera cautiously approached the animal.

"How did you get here, big fellow?" Heera asked,

sitting on his haunches a few yards away from the pit.

The elephant sat up, as if injected with new hope. Its eyes were tired but soft with both fear and anticipation. Heera knew it wouldn't hurt him. Perhaps this was the certainty of naivety, but he knew it to be true. Lowering himself into the pit, he slipped and landed in the water with a splash.

"Look what you've got me into," he said, rubbing his eyes to squeeze the water out. "Stand up. You don't think I can lift you out like a baby, do you?" Heera slapped the elephant's bottom gently. "Come on. Up on your feet. I'll try and push you."

The elephant – even though it was a baby – was obviously too heavy for a little boy to push out and, too soon, it became clear that the idea was not a brilliant one. Heera looked around and, like lightning, a thought came whizzing into his head.

He crawled out of the pit where a banyan tree stood a few metres away. Grabbing one of its aerial roots, he tugged at it, to assess its strength. It felt robust and looked long enough to reach the elephant. Heera walked to the pit holding onto the loose end of the root.

"Here you go," he offered, throwing the root at the animal's trunk. "Come on. Grab it and get out of there."

The elephant was far too distressed and didn't

seem to know what to do.

"Come on big fellow," Heera encouraged. "You have to help yourself. Take it." He wrapped the root around his hand. "Like this, you see. And wrap it with your trunk."

The elephant took the root in its trunk and held it limply.

"Well done, dost," Heera cheered. "Pull. Like this." He beckoned, tugging at the root while the elephant held it with its trunk.

The elephant calf didn't pull. It was confused and trying to gain a purchase in the mud.

"Come on. I can't be pulling a big baby like you out of this," Heera urged the animal who still didn't pull. "What do you think I am? *Bajrang Bali?*"

Somehow, the elephant stabilised itself on its four feet and looped the root around its trunk a couple of times, then heaved to gain leverage. The root went taut, burning Heera's palms where he was still holding on. He flinched and let go. The banyan tree shook with the weight of the animal.

"COME ON," Heera cheered and clapped, despite the pain in his palms. He jumped up and down with joy.

The elephant calf's feet slipped on the soil, as they tried hard to gain a firm hold on the ground. Heera got into the pit behind it and patted the flank of the animal to encourage it.

"Go, go, go," he cried.

The elephant trumpeted with the effort and, in a few minutes, it had hauled itself up and out of the pit.

"Hurray!" screamed Heera, throwing his hands up in the air and splashing around in the water in the pit.

The elephant rolled up its trunk and let out an exuberant cry.

Heera rammed his fingertips into his ears.

The animal turned around to Heera, still in the pit.

"You're magnificent!" Heera crooned.

The elephant walked around the edges of the pit, stopping here and there, to find a spot where it could anchor its feet without falling back in.

"Hey! What do you want now?"

Heera had expected it to leave but instead the grateful animal lowered its trunk to grab Heera.

"What – what are you doing?" Heera's voice rose in panic. But the elephant's touch was gentle. It reached Heera's waist, wrapping its trunk around it, and effortlessly picked him up and out of the pit. "Woah! Careful," Heera shrieked in excitement tinted with fear, feeling the warm, wrinkled skin of the trunk on his bare upper body. He was placed tenderly on the ground. "Ah! That was handy. Thank you, dost." Heera stroked the elephant's forehead,

18

cringing with pain as his bruised palms rubbed against the animal's coarse hide.

The elephant stood about five feet tall and towered above Heera who was around a foot shorter. It looped its trunk around Heera's arm. Heera felt its balminess and strength once again.

"You're strong. Just like Bajrang Bali." He paused at an idea that had just sped across his mind. "I have a name for you," he declared. "Let's call you *Bali* for short. Bali. Bali." He repeated the name, feeling the sound of it, then asked the animal, "Do you like it?"

Bali was clueless that he'd earned himself a name. But he knew he'd made a new friend. Someone who had saved his life. Someone he could trust. And someone to whom he would be eternally grateful.

"Done. Carved in stone. From today you're named Bali," Heera said grandly. "Oh! And by the way, I'm Heera…" He pointed to his lips and said, "HEE-RAA."

The rain had stopped, leaving the ground sodden and slushy. Heera picked up a stick and drew a diamond shape in the soggy earth where they stood.

"Look. This is a heera. That's what my name means. Get it?" he asked and chuckled. "You're Bali, and I'm Heera". He looked at the elephant's forehead. It had a patch of skin in a shade that stood out on the animal's grey body – an inverted triangle of pinkish beige. "I like that. You look like a prince with a crown." He lifted his right arm to expose the inside of his upper arm, a few inches above his elbow, and held it up. "Look, I too have a mark on my body. It's a tattoo. Can you see?" Bali put his trunk to Heera's arm as if sniffing it. "No. It's not a real scorpion, silly. This one has four pincers, unlike the real ones. Look. It's a ritual." Heera swung his arm down forcefully so that it swayed back with the momentum of its weight and then forward. He kept swinging it up and down as he spoke. "Ma says every member of a family in our tribe gets a tattoo that is special to that family. Every family has a unique design. But we don't live with our tribe anymore. Ma says they banished her because she married my father. He didn't belong to the tribe. And he died only a few years after I was born." Bali only blinked. "Anyways, that's a different story. Even Ma has one like this on her upper arm. It's so that we recognise each other when we leave our bodies behind and enter the spirit world. Isn't that both silly *and* wonderful?" Heera giggled. "I told Ma it was silly because how would we have our tattoos when we leave our bodies? They'd stay behind too. But she says these tattoos remain engraved on our souls. I know it's not like yours. It's not natural. They use thorns to cut the skin and then they mix soot with animal fat to fill in the deep blue colour. Ma also told me that it was very painful because the wound is supposed to get infected so the tattoos become larger, darker and clearer. I know, it all sounds too horrible. But she says it should be done. It's better than getting lost in the spirit world. But I'm lucky I don't remember any of it because it was all done when I was barely a year old." Heera beamed and jumped up, excited. "Oh! I know – that's *your* family's unique design, then?"

The elephant blinked.

"Where is your herd?" A sadness tugged at Heera's heart as he realised the animal had somehow been separated from its mother. "You're lost…aren't you?" Heera stroked its forehead. He felt a guttural growl rise from deep within the elephant. "You must miss your Ma so much. But don't you worry. I'll be there for you –"

Heera stopped mid-sentence, remembering that his mother would have returned home by now and would panic not finding him there.

"Oh no…I've to go. See you soon, dost." He dashed in the direction of the hut, not stopping once to look back.

When he got home, Heera had to face a stormy mother, who was terrified, furious, and happy all at once. Heera got hugged first and then kissed and then yelled at. And once the maternal storm of fury had abated, the mother and son found a juvenile, elephant standing right outside their hut. And that is how a new friendship was born between boy and animal.

Chapter Three

Heera woke up in his hut. His eyes rolled back, unmoored by the concussion. There was nothing but blankness for a few fleeting seconds. The roof of the hut appeared blurred then quickly came into focus. And then everything came rushing back – the sahib's smug face, the screams, the trumpeting, Bali's bobbing head.

"BALI. BALI!" Heera sat up screaming with a hand over his head where the blow from the rifle had left a swollen, blue bruise.

Vasu jumped in her skin, dropping an earthen pot. It shattered into thousands of pieces. Unheeding, she ran to Heera and threw herself down on the floor next to him.

"Heera, my child."

"Ma, where is Bali?"

Vasu embraced Heera in a fierce hug. "Thank

God you're all right."

While collecting wood, she had strayed into that part of the forest where Bali had been caught – although a few hours later – to find her son lying unconscious. Horror-struck, she had thrown down the bundle of wood and carried Heera home in her lean but muscular arms.

"How did you hurt yourself?" Vasu held her hands in a namaste, looking up at the heavens. "Thank you, Shiva, for sending me there. How else would I have known where to find my child?" She looked at Heera. "You could have–" She trailed off, unable to speak her fears out loud.

Vasu smelled of ashes and earth and for a moment Heera relaxed in her comforting and familiar embrace, but the next he began resisting her.

"Where is Bali?" he asked, trying to fight his way out of her embrace. Her hold was strong but gentle. "Tell me. Where is he?" Panic surged in his throat.

"Bali? Calm down, my child." Vasu cupped his face in her palms; the skin on them was leathery from carrying firewood every day for the last umpteen years. However, these hands seasoned in toil also had a sure tenderness about them. She forced his reluctant head down on her chest. "Now tell me what happened. What about Bali?"

"Bali – the gunshot – Bali was caught – I saw that white man." Heera babbled in the same terror-struck tone.

"Bali? White man?" Vasu had heard the gunshot that day, like many more before. Realisation dawned on her. "Oh God! Was it Bali?" Vasu sighed. "Oh, Heera!" She turned Heera's face towards her. He didn't look her in the eye. "What happened, child? Were you there when–?" She didn't dare complete her sentence.

Heera nodded. "I saw him being lassoed by the shikaris."

He told her everything that had happened.

"He hit you? He hit my child? That monster!" A burst of fury made her cheeks burn.

"Ma, I must find out where Bali is. I have to. I need to. Will you help me?"

Vasu remained silent and hugged him again.

Heera shrugged her away. "Have they killed him? Is that what it is? Is that why you're not answering me?"

Vasu looked away and stood up. She didn't like Heera to see her cry. But she couldn't help the tears welling up in her eyes. She feared Bali dead, knowing most animals were hunted down to be killed. But how could she reveal her fears? She struggled for composure and quickly flicked the tears away.

The silence was deafening to Heera. He stood up and rushed to her and shook her by the arm.

"Speak up, Ma."

Vasu cleared her throat and straightened her voice. "My child, I can only tell you what I think might have happened.... But it may not be true." She wrapped her arms around Heera who, at age thirteen, was now as tall as her.

"Tell me what you *think* then. Don't be silent. It's killing me."

"The truth is I don't know... but you know how the sahibs are." She spoke warily, weighing every word.

Heera felt his blood run cold.

"But he may well be alive," she quickly added. "There is no reason to assume his death, especially if you haven't seen it happen."

The nasty face of the British officer flashed before Heera's eyes. His breath quickened and his upper lip started to bead with sweat. "But what if he is?"

Heera felt his world implode within. Tears rolled down his cheeks.

Vasu stroked his hair. "He may still be alive. There's still hope, my dear. Don't give it up. It's the only thing we have." She lifted his head up high and kissed his forehead and wiped his tears. "Come," she said, gently pulling him towards the corner of the hut that held pots and pans. She sat him down there and went to fetch a basket. "Here, first eat something." She held out a bunch of gooseberries in front of him. "You need to heal, son, and get some strength."

The berries reminded Heera of his benevolent friend. Burrowing his face into his knees, he sobbed and sobbed until there were no tears left to shed.

Vasu didn't stop him. She sat next to him and held him close and let him be. It was best sometimes to let it all out, she knew. She'd been there before. Letting the tears wash away the raw pain helped to make space for courage, strength, and hope.

Chapter Four

A scrawny little baby sat on top of a neem tree, bawling away like crazy when Heera arrived. How had the baby got up there? The baby shrieked louder on seeing Heera and tried to crawl along the branch that careened perilously.

Heera's insides turned icy thinking about the baby striking the rocky floor several feet below. It felt as if a part of him was crawling up there. Unfathomable fear gripped him.

He strained and tried to climb the tree with all his might but to his surprise he couldn't find a foot hold or gain a purchase. The tree trunk was as smooth and glossy as marble even though it looked pretty much like any other neem tree.

The baby looked like it was in pain and kept rubbing its arm.

If he couldn't get up there, then he could catch

the baby if it fell or jumped.

"Come to me," Heera called softly, but the words didn't come out at all. Only his lips moved. His voice was lost. He cleared his throat and tried again but it was pointless. His vocal cords were on strike.

Heera didn't feel like himself. What was going on?

The howling infant swayed sideways. Heera cringed and braced himself to catch him. But the baby stayed put, stuck its tongue out and kicked out its dangling leg at Heera, as if mocking him.

Strangely, although the branch the baby was on was at least ten feet up, the baby's ankle dangled like a pendulum, right in front of Heera's face. And on the chubby brown ankle sat a silver anklet.

Heera woke in a sudden panic and sat bolt upright. He had been dreaming about the child with the anklet. Again.

Vasu wasn't next to him. It was early morning and she'd left to collect wood.

Although his dreams would change a bit here and there, some in the forest, some at the river, some outside his hut, all of them had the same howling child with the silver anklet on its right ankle, and all of them made him ache with vulnerability and powerlessness.

Heera had told his mother numerous times about

the dream, but Vasu would never acknowledge it; always brushed it away.

Most times, she'd say something like, *It's just a dream. There's nothing else to it*, and quickly move on to some other topic.

Heera wiped his upper lip, dripping with sweat, onto the back of his arm.

Bird song had just begun. Through the little window in the wall of his hut, Heera could see the sky exploding in a blaze of pink and gold, gushing its way through the violet that had dominated it hours ago.

The image of Bali came whirling into his head and now he wished he could still be asleep, despite the dream. It was far better than bearing the pang of longing which grew within him.

Heera left for the forest. It was his second mother. In its lap he felt at home – its placid and lively presence soothing his spirit. And he needed it more than ever today.

Not knowing if Bali was alive was excruciatingly painful. Perhaps more than knowing he was dead.

There was not one place or thing that didn't remind him of Bali. The fruits reminded him of the fruits Bali used to get him. The trees reminded him of the games he played with Bali. The river retold the countless water-fights and mud-baths they had together. The air in the forest smelled like Bali and summoned memories. And those memories stung.

Wandering aimlessly, not knowing what to do next or where to find Bali, he sat atop a huge banyan tree with his arms wrapped around a thick branch, cheek resting on the coarse bark. Taking in the fragrance of earthy, green wood, he hoped to find some respite from the haunting memories.

Trees were as alive as humans to him, except they had a candour more distinct than most human beings possessed. And he loved banyan trees since he could swing on their prop roots, but the one he was sitting on in particular was his favourite.

It was the tree, the roots of which he had used to rescue a much younger Bali from the water-flooded pit. It was the spot where he had met Bali for the very first time. This tree had an intricate network of strong supporting structures, resembling pillars, that were actually roots which the tree had sent down. These pillars were stalwart and resembled new tree trunks, except that they appeared to be made from many finer root-like structures, heavily interwoven and stuck together. It had given Heera ample space to play hide-and-seek with Bali.

A memory came flashing to him. "Bali. Catch me," he had shouted, throwing himself recklessly off a branch about four metres above the ground.

Within a fraction of a second, Bali's trunk had gripped Heera, catching him cleanly before he could hit the ground. The emotion was so intense, Heera could feel the warmth of Bali's trunk, even as he was reliving the memory. It was a security and trust unlike any he had known. No matter how he jumped, he was always caught.

Once Bali had been jabbed on his flank by a pointy and stout branch sticking out at a perilous angle while catching Heera. Bali had bled profusely and Heera had cried and apologised and cursed himself for days for making Bali suffer.

"Forgive me, Bali. I promise I will never let this happen to you again. I will never let you get hurt again. I promise." Heera had said the thousandth time in a week, stroking Bali's forehead. And Bali had discreetly snaked his trunk behind Heera and playfully nudged his bottom with it. Heera had noticed the golden-brown eyes, twinkling with mischief.

The memory was so vivid, a smile escaped Heera's lips. Pleasant for a brief moment, and aching the very next, his insides weighed down with a heaviness that came down on him like a wet blanket. The promise he had made resounded in his ears. He hadn't been able to save his friend. He hadn't kept his word. He had broken a promise.

Holding out the sickle he would usually take along into the forest for defending himself, in case he needed to, he squinted at its glinting blade.

Without further thought, he held his shoulderlength hair against the blade and started to hack at it. The angle was inconvenient but soon he got through the bunches of hair and then let them go. Tufts of hair, a good few inches long, cascaded into his lap. Heera hewed and hewed as close to his scalp as he could with the sickle until it became tiresome to continue.

There! This is for you, Bali. I'll never grow them until I get you back.

Chapter Five

Heera barely ate or drank anything and spent the next few days in a cloud of despair. He was everything to Vasu and it broke her heart to see the apple of her eye in agony. She hadn't liked his hair long but now she didn't like it short. It was a constant reminder of her child's anguish.

She coaxed him to come with her to the bazaar, hoping it would act as a distraction. She also promised she'd get him his favourite Indian sweet, jalebee, to cheer him up.

Vasu didn't remember the last time she had eaten a jalebee herself. The saffron in the jalebee was an expensive ingredient and she couldn't afford the indulgence. However, every year, at least once on Diwali, she would ensure that Heera was fed jalebees. She'd feel like a queen that day, buying her son what he loved. But, of course, those days were rare and precious.

This day wasn't Diwali day, although it was an exception. Heera's smile was priceless to her. She tried not to think too much about the extra money needed for the jalebees. Skipping a meal would make up for the cost of them, she decided.

The bazaar was a crowded, noisy, and vibrantly colourful place, teeming with the aroma of flowers, spices, and the smell of tobacco. Heera had seen it before, but it had been a while. He wasn't fond of the bazaar. It was a place with too many people. Too many people judging and frowning and hissing at him. Animals were better. At least they didn't care how someone dressed and how much money someone had. He preferred the jungle; chaotic but beautiful, forbidding but just, fierce but calm, all at the same time. It welcomed anyone walking into it with open arms.

He looked at the rows of shops that ran parallel to each other, with a vast array of things on sale; some selling spices, condiments, and chillies stacked in colourful conical heaps, some selling fragrant flowers and garlands, some selling fruits, clothes, carpets, and toys and some selling sweet meats and earthen pots and pans.

The gaps in between the rows were filled with men and women, rushing around from shop to shop in sarees and turbans, buying and bargaining with merchants. The rich, although only a few, sashayed around in their fine robes, jingling coins in their purses, fussing over what to buy. Children scampered about, squealing in joy, some imploring their parents to buy bits and pieces, some mooching about the shops, getting told off by merchants. Hawkers shouted out special offers on their products, enticing people passing by to purchase stuff. A drunken man lurched along the streets blabbering to himself. Dogs, cows, goats, and chicken meandered around aimlessly, although some of them were on sale and harnessed to poles with ropes or caged. Beggars hobbled about with their bowls, in anticipation of getting a paisa or two. All in all, it looked like a kaleidoscope of chaos, colour, sound, and smell all intertwined.

"This way, son," Vasu said, gently pulling Heera by his arm. "The sweet shop there has excellent jalebees." She gestured to a shop at the end of the row where they had been walking.

Heera's feet dragged; the jalebees were the last thing on his mind. His appetite had left with Bali. But he hadn't bothered arguing with Mother. It was an arduous task. He had to choose his battles. Not all could be won. This time he decided to give in.

As they walked, he noticed a shop selling wooden toys, ahead on his left. The shopkeeper was out of sight, Heera noticed, when a boy around his age picked up a black slate and piece of chalk and drew something on it. Heera's eyes followed the stretched-out rope on the boy's arm. It ended around the neck of a monkey; a white-face macaque with bright eyes, busy devouring an apple. The monkey looked at Heera with attentive eyes, gnawing at the fruit greedily.

"Get away, you little runt." The shopkeeper came out staggering as fast as he could. It was an effort to get his corpulent body to move swiftly.

The boy jumped back, throwing the slate and chalk piece at the shopkeeper. The macaque's mouth tensed.

"Keep your hair on, fatso. Just trying it out… not stealing," the boy teased and twisted his face into an ugly grimace at the shopkeeper before propelling himself through the crowd with the macaque on his shoulder.

"You dare come here again –" shouted the shopkeeper after him, but the boy was gone. "The rascal." The shopkeeper scowled and picked up the slate. The side the boy had doodled on happened to face Heera.

Heera glanced at the slate. And froze.

Vasu tugged at Heera's arm and he carried on – in a daze. Was it what he thought it was? Had the boy really drawn what he thought he had? Was he hallucinating, dreaming? It had to be his imagination.

Perhaps a trick of light or his own mind. After all, he hadn't been sleeping well.

"Come, we're not far," Vasu beckoned and walked on ahead of her son. "Almost there."

But Heera had stopped in his tracks. His feet took him towards the toy shop where the boy had been doodling over the slate.

"Oi, what do you want?" the shopkeeper snapped, goggling at Heera's tatty garments.

Heera's eyes remained glued to the slate. The hair on his nape prickled.

"Are you deaf? Can't you hear me? I don't want little rascals like you around my shop," the man rattled on.

Heera was covered in goose bumps. He wasn't dreaming. He looked up at the shopkeeper. He hadn't heard a word of what the man had been saying.

"Who was that boy?" Heera asked, an urgency ringing in his voice.

"Boy? What boy?"

Heera pointed to the slate.

"That little runt? A thief... obviously... how do I know who he was? Don't waste my time. I'm here to sell toys." The shopkeeper paused to look at Heera top to toe, then said, "I don't suppose you can buy any. Get away from my shop. We don't entertain beggars."

Heera frowned at his arrogance. He had a good mind to throw one of the wooden elephants that were on display at the shopkeeper's head, but the elephant reminded him of Bali and the pang of longing to see his friend intensified. He turned with a heavy heart and walked away in the direction of where Vasu had headed.

A distant but sharp rattle of a damru caught his attention.

A penetrating, young voice shouted out, "Listen up! Listen up, everybody! Listen up close." The rattle of the damru came again. "Come over, everybody! Come over. Come closer." Another bright and sharp rattling followed. "Come over, people! The rich, the poor, the young and the old, ladies and gentlemen. Do yourself a favour. Come watch the show! Make your day!"

It came from the main market square where a crowd was beginning to form.

There was a ripple of excitement in the bazaar. Heera overheard a few children talking.

"Hey, let's go quick."

"It's the monkey boy. Come on."

"I've heard about it. Can't wait to see for myself. Come on, quick."

The boy with the monkey flashed in front of Heera's eyes. Could it be him?

Vasu had already walked a considerable distance

before she noticed Heera's absence next to her.

"Heera! Where are you?" She whipped around to find him looking in the opposite direction. "Come on, what are you looking at?"

Vasu's shout jolted Heera out of his trance; however, he ignored her; his senses still fastened to the scene. "Ma, can we go there?"

Vasu shook her head in disapproval. "I thought we were getting *jalebees*." But, noticing Heera's falling countenance, she quickly agreed. "Okay. Let's go. But we can't be leaving the show without paying the monkey's owner. It won't be fair. And we won't be left with money for enough jalebees. We can get one or two at the most. Is that okay?"

The sweet aroma of sugar, ghee and the fragrance of saffron was too strong to ignore anymore. On any other day, it would have floored Heera, but not this day. He didn't care whether they bought any or not.

He nodded. "Come on, then. Let's go." He ran towards the main market square while Vasu struggled to keep up with his pace.

"Heera," she called. "Slow down, son." Her voice sank in the mayhem of sounds. But Heera ran, hope burning within him. He had to dig deeper.

The market square was an open area surrounded by street hawkers and food stalls and bullock carts and horse carts. It was as busy around the edges of the market square as the other parts of the bazaar except that everything avoided this central area, as if an invisible force kept everything out on purpose, unless there was a street show going on.

The clatter of the damru got louder and louder as Heera approached the throng of people.

"Come on, people! Say hello to Basanti. Basanti, bow down to everyone." The voice was tireless and hammy; every word vibrating with energy. Loud and clear and sharp.

All Heera could see above the heads of the people was a hand held high with a damru between its fingers spinning madly on its wrist. Vasu was somewhere far behind. Heera, being tall for his age, found it easy to jostle his way through to the front to take a closer look.

His eyes fell on a monkey standing up on its rear legs in the centre of the crowd. The monkey brought its palms together and bowed down to the crowd in a namaste. The crowd cheered.

Heera was pretty sure it was the macaque he had seen moments ago. Unlike most humans, he was good at telling one animal from the other.

"Well done, Basanti! Good girl."

Heera followed the voice and saw the boy at the edge of the mob. It was undeniably the same boy who had doodled on the slate moments ago. Heera's eyes lit up.

The macaque bowed in a namaste in every

direction.

"Come on, people. She deserves a round of applause!" The crowd cheered and clapped. The boy held out a piece of fruit to his pet. The macaque smacked its lips, pulled its ears back and raised its brows.

"Now, Basanti. Let's show them what you can do," the boy said theatrically. "She's no ordinary monkey. She's a wonder girl! Yes, she is!" he told the crowd.

The crowd rejoiced. Children squealed in glee and anticipation. The old and the young were all amused and intrigued.

"Okay, so I need a volunteer." The boy pivoted on his heels to scan the whole crowd around him. "One volunteer. Come on! Who's the lucky one? Step forward!"

People looked at each other, some contemplating if they should go, some too shy. A few raised their hands but before anybody else could move, a little girl – around half Heera's age – stepped forward.

"I'll do it," she said, blushing pink.

"What's your name, little one?" the boy asked, kneeling beside her.

"Mina," she mumbled.

"Okay, ladies and gentlemen," he said, standing back up and throwing his hands out as if presenting Mina to the audience as a gift. "Here is little Mina who will be my assistant! She'll lock this trunk here and keep the key with her." He pointed to a rusty-looking trunk with a lock and key on top of its lid.

The boy gave her the lock and key. "Okay, Mina. Now you lock it and keep hold of the key. Can you do that?" Mina nodded. "Go on, then."

After a bit of fiddling around, Mina locked the trunk and kept the key. "Hold it out so everyone can see it." The boy ushered. Mina held out the key.

The boy jiggled the lock. "Okay. It's locked. She has the key." He pointed at Mina. "Can everyone see?" The boy pivoted on his heels again to face his audience in all directions. He gestured to Mina to lower her hand. "You can keep it with you for now and step aside." He smiled at her. "Now watch what my wonder girl Basanti can do. She's going to open the lock without the key!" The boy spoke the last sentence very slowly for dramatic effect.

The crowd gasped. Waves of excitement stirred the throng. The macaque sat quietly, opening and closing its mouth, rapidly extending and retracting the tongue alternately.

"Mina, can I borrow one of your hair pins?" the boy asked. Mina tugged at her hair and pulled out a pin. "This is an ordinary hair pin." He held out the pin to the crowd. "Now look carefully what Basanti will do. Show them, Basanti." He lowered the pin to Basanti, who was waving her tail playfully from side to side. She took the pin, ears flapping forward and back, and went to the trunk. After inserting the pin, she crouched low to hear, as if listening intently.

The crowd was muted, excitement throbbing in the silence. All eyes were on Basanti, including Mina's and Heera's.

After a few minutes the macaque raised her head and grunted. The lock clicked open. She picked it up and held it out to the boy.

"She's done it!" The boy brandished the lock.

The mob applauded and whistled with exhilaration. The boy rewarded the monkey with a whole pear.

"Well done, my wonder girl!" The boy raised his hands and joined the audience in applauding Basanti, who again bowed down with a namaste to the crowd.

Next, the boy asked for another volunteer.

A man hesitantly stepped forward.

The boy gave him a puppet made out of fabric and wood, around a foot tall.

"Can you please sit down and hold the puppet upright? Be steady and don't panic," he told the man. "Just hold it away from your body."

The man did as he was told.

"Basanti is also a warrior," the boy declared. "Watch closely everyone!"

Basanti had finished the pear.

"Okay, Basanti. Are you ready, girl?"

The macaque discarded the core of the pear and looked at him attentively, ears forward.

"Attack!" The boy pointed at the puppet.

Basanti pounced onto the puppet. She smacked it couple of times and bit into it, ripping the cloth.

"Spin kick!" the boy shouted.

Basanti spun around and kicked the puppet. The man holding it dropped the puppet nervously and fell back.

"Doesn't she deserve a round of applause! She's a star, isn't she? Basanti, ladies and gentlemen!" The macaque bowed once again in a namaste.

The crowd went wild.

"Now if you'd be kind enough to part with some annas." With both hands the boy held out a drawstring bag made with a ragged piece of cloth and handed it to the macaque who held it open and walked around the circle of people to collect coins.

People, especially at the back, started to shuffle around and move away to escape the situation and avoid paying the boy.

Heera realised he didn't have any money on him. Mother wasn't around and, even if she was, he didn't want to ask her now that he had found the boy. So, he sneaked out, shame thumping his chest.

"Heera," Vasu called from somewhere, hoping to find him as the show ended. She still hadn't seen him, but Heera spotted her just in time to escape. He ducked under the crowd and ran to a nearby shop, then hid behind a hanging carpet that was on display. He decided to elude his mother, because he had to pursue this boy and find out more about what he had seen him draw.

After the crowd dispersed, Heera saw the boy walking towards a fruit shop a few rows down from where they were.

The fruit shop had banana bunches hanging from the ceiling. A scaffolding made of bamboo with a white canvas stretched across it made a canopy over the shop.

The boy was looking around furtively.

Vasu called again and Heera stayed put where he was. When he was sure she'd left he sneaked out and went towards the fruit shop. But the boy he had seen moments ago was suddenly nowhere to be seen. Heera ran towards the shop and looked around but could see nobody. The canopy was big and below it sat heaps of fruit; pomegranates, chikoos, custard apples, and many more.

A girl in a worn blue skirt and blouse, suddenly stood up from behind one of these fruit stacks, fanning herself with half a banana leaf, still looking down. Two black braids dangled to her waist from behind her ears. Her brows were thick, although scanty where they met at the centre of her forehead.

Sweat made her bronze skin glisten.

"Take it… it's fine… I told you," she said, looking down. "I can handle Appa… I'll make something up… leave it to me. Just take it, will you?"

She noticed Heera in her peripheral vision and looked up at him, beaming with the enthusiasm of finding a prospective customer. "A dozen pomegranates for the price of ten. Only 8 annas," she said to him. "Would you like some?"

Heera stared back mutely. Did she look like someone he knew? But he hardly knew any girls or, for that matter, anyone except his mother and Bali and the wildlife.

"Or half dozen for the price of five? Yes? No?" She nodded and shook her head, miming for each option. Then she gestured to her ears and shook her head again, assuming he was deaf and dumb.

Heera was about to ask if she'd seen the boy he had seen moments ago when the boy himself stood up right next to the girl, holding bunches of bananas. Basanti the macaque was sitting on his shoulders and eating one, cooing with joy.

"Maya, are you sure?" he asked in Hindi before Heera could even open his mouth.

Seeing him up close, he noticed the boy had chestnut-brown eyes that stood out on his dark-brown skin. The boy's eyes were striking to him, something about them vaguely familiar. They were much like Bali's, Heera decided, and then chucked the thought away. He was being ridiculous. Everything and everyone had something to do with Bali. He was losing it. *Focus. What are you here for?*

"Of course, Raju." The girl fiercely nodded at him. It was the Indian nod, in which the head went side to side. Raju smiled briefly. "How many times will you ask the same question?"

"Hey, you," Heera stuttered, struggling to speak.

"Oh! You talk!!" Maya clapped her hands and gave a hoot of laughter. Dimples appeared on both her cheeks and deepened when she bared her teeth.

Heera ignored her. His eyes were fixed on the boy. How had he made that figure on the slate? He had to find out.

"Hey, you, what have you been drawing there?" he finally asked.

Raju looked puzzled. "Are you talking to me?"

"Yes – to you – there – over there." Heera pointed to the toy shop.

"Drawing? What drawing?" Raju screwed his eyes. And then it struck him. How could this boy have noticed what he drew? He tried to look casual. "I don't know what you're talking about." He gave out a hollow giggle.

"There at the shop – on the slate – I saw you—"

"What did you see?" Raju snapped back. "I don't even know what you mean."

"Where did you learn to do that?"

"And who are you to come here investigating who did what and where?" Maya countered.

Heera clicked his tongue and started to scan the ground.

A flash of recognition lit Maya's eyes, as if a veil was lifted making her see what she had been blind to just moments ago. She blushed.

Heera bent down and picked up a small flat stone with a sharp, pointed edge.

"Please. This is important. Look." He sat down on his haunches and carved a shape into the soil.

Maya stepped out and looked at the ground, and Raju followed.

"Look." Heera pointed to the ground. "You made that there, didn't you? I know you did."

"I – no, I didn't – why would I?" A disconcerted look, that Heera caught, flashed across Raju's face. "Never seen that." Raju shrugged his shoulders. "I think you're delusional."

"I know what I saw," Heera snapped back.

"It's just a drawing. What's the big deal?"

"Raju… calm down," Maya urged. She looked at Heera's face again, and her gaze ducked as soon as Heera caught it.

"It's a drawing, yes… but it means a lot to me." Heera clenched his fists and tried to restrain his temper that was beginning to surge. "This… it's my name... it means *me*."

"You?" Maya looked puzzled.

"Yes... I'm Heera." He looked at Raju who was looking a little nervous and said, "You know what heera means, don't you?"

"Who doesn't?" Maya blushed, tucking a stray strand of hair behind her ear.

Raju looked at her crossly, as if to say, *What's wrong with you?* And then flicked his eyes back at Heera. "What are you going on about?" he asked.

"This was something I taught Bali to draw. I—" Heera often spoke about Bali like he was a person, almost always forgetting that he was an elephant.

"Who's Bali?" Raju asked, cutting him off.

"My dost – an elephant. He was caught a few days ago."

Raju's heart skipped a beat on hearing the word '*elephant*'.

Maya shifted with unease. "Raju—" she said but was hushed brusquely by Raju who turned his back to Heera and glowered.

"It was something I taught him to draw – Bali knew how to do this. He would draw my name *exactly* like this." Heera looked at the shape he had etched below in the earth. "Nobody else could have known unless—" He broke off to look up at Raju from the ground. "–unless he's seen Bali do it. Which means that Bali *is* alive." Heera felt a surge of hope swelling in his chest, the last word reverberating. *Alive. Bali is alive.* "Have you seen him?" he asked cautiously, dreading the reply would be negative.

"Elephants drawing... amusing." Raju bent down and held out another banana to his macaque – who now sat at his feet – to avoid Heera's eyes, and let out an empty chuckle. "Never seen one myself."

Maya's eyes were fixed on Raju in a kind of livid stare.

All the hope bled away. Heera bit his lip as if to hold on to a last drop of it. *He's alive. Bali is alive.* He cast Raju a look of suspicion. "Are you sure?"

Maya looked disconcertedly at Heera, wrapping one of her braids around her index finger.

"Goodness, I actually forgot. I have to go now," Raju said ignoring his question. He straightened up and looked at Maya, with an urgency in his tone.

"Can you come inside for a second?" she said, brimming with a mixture of surprise and exasperation.

"Er – I don't want any more, Maya." Raju held up his bunch of bananas. "Basanti has had a few now."

"Come *here*," Maya said slowly, emphasizing every word, accompanying them with a made-up smile, and went into the canopy.

"What are you looking at? I told you I know

nothing of an elephant. Leave us alone now, will you?" Raju chided Heera and stepped inside the canopy.

Heera peered after the pair, then turned his back on them and walked away, downcast.

"What is the matter with you?" Maya hissed. "Why are you lying to his face?"

"Keep shut, Maya—"

"But why?"

A surge of sounds, sensations and colours crowded his mind; the lash of a cane, a sharp crack, a stinging burn across his palm, red, blue, purple, screaming pain. He flinched and closed his fist, digging his nails deeper into his clammy palms.

"I can't." Raju hung his head. "Don't – don't say a word to him." He picked up the bananas. "I'll take these. Shukriya." Raju looked at Basanti. "*Ketch, ketch,*" he called, clicking his tongue against his palate. The macaque hopped onto his shoulder and Raju walked away.

Maya stomped out of the canopy after him, brows crossed tightly. She caught a glimpse of Heera who was about to disappear amongst a crowd of people. Hitching up her skirt, she ran to him.

"Hey! Stop! Heera!"

She ran into the crowd, trying not to lose sight of him. Heera stopped and turned abruptly, causing Maya to almost bump into him.

Looking at him closely, she noticed a wafer-thin layer of hair on his upper lip. A year had changed him enough to make him almost unrecognisable for a couple of minutes. She caught herself staring and dropped her eyes, flushing into a fiery shade of bronze-orange.

"What is it?" Heera asked.

"You don't recognise me, do you?" she asked and, without stopping for an answer as was customary, she continued. "Never mind. Follow Raju and you might find what you're looking for."

Heera forgot her question instantly. "You mean, Bali?"

Maya nodded. "The elephant might be Bali from what you told us." She smiled.

A rush of joy to his head made Heera dizzy for an instant. Bali wasn't dead after all. And in another second, the lie uttered by Raju made him wild with ire. "He lied? *Why*?"

"Perhaps because Major Crook–" She flicked her brows up and down.

"Who's Major Crook?"

"He's the one who caught Bali! But there's no time to waste. Follow him. He's going straight there. That's why he took the bananas." She spoke hurriedly. "Go now. You can follow him. He's gone that way." She darted in Raju's direction. "Come," she called.

53

Heera's heart danced with glee. He ran after her.

Soon, she pointed at Raju's back in the distance. "There he is," she said, catching her breath. "Go."

Heera turned to her with gratitude. "You don't know what this means to me. Thank you!" Holding on to the flicker of hope with all his heart, he ran.

Chapter Six

In an archetypal bungalow built from brick and stone, with a stark whitewashed finish, lived Major Crook – a man of dark thoughts and dark intentions. The bungalow had a hipped roof and was situated in a large, landscaped compound to the west of the forest, although not very far from it. It was a low, one-storey, spacious building, having a symmetrical internal layout: a hall in the centre, rooms on each side, a veranda all around, and a garden in the front.

Crook was relatively new to the town and was served by an entourage of Indian servants, many of whom had served him for years. They moved with him wherever he went. The servants' quarters were detached and located behind the main house. The entire set-up reflected the sheer contrast of the lifestyles of the natives and the rulers.

A few days ago, Raju, a servant boy living in the servants' quarters, had heard rumours about an elephant that Major Crook had captured. He had to see it.

The Major was known for hunting animals for sport, but what intrigued Raju was this one had been captured and not killed. And although he was glad about it, he wondered why.

"What do you think, Basanti? Should we ask Baba? Maybe he can take us to see the elephant," he had asked his pet macaque. Basanti cocked her head and her bright eyes set attentively on Raju's face. "I'll take that as a yes."

Rajveer – or Baba as Raju called him – was an old, retired soldier, who now did miscellaneous tasks in and around the bungalow. Right from assisting the khansama, to polishing the Major's shoes, to washing, cleaning, weeding the lawns and trimming the hedge, there was nothing he hadn't done. He was a jack of all trades, used more like a stepney, covering for any sick servants as and when required, or assisting when nobody needed covering for. In return he had been given a roof over his head at the servants' quarters and the security of three meals a day. And of course, he was paid wages, which were meagre and as good as nothing.

"Yes. They've captured an elephant," Rajveer had confirmed.

"Take me there, Baba, please. I would like to see it."

"I can't do that. You know the Major. It's not our business, Raju."

Raju's excitement came crashing down from his head to his heels. He realised he couldn't put Rajveer in trouble just because he was curious. After all, Baba was everything to him.

Rajveer had raised Raju as his own child after finding him abandoned as a baby on the riverbank in a neighbouring town. Having lost his wife and child during childbirth decades before, he saw Raju as godsent: a boon to him. Raju filled the void in Rajveer's life, although he was too old to be a father and was more like a grandfather.

"Hey, look here, my little langoor. You look terrible when you sulk," Rajveer teased, his eyes twinkling. His copious white beard, bushy white eyebrows and enormous white moustache all moved as he spoke, as if they were doing the talking. "How do you expect Basanti to think you're handsome if you look like that? After all she'd want a good-looking husband. No?"

"Cheee, I'm not marrying Basanti!" Raju nudged Rajveer in the side with his elbow. Rajveer roared with an earth-shaking laughter that shook his belly; it was big enough to fit a rhino. He looked like Santa Claus's brown-skinned cousin.

Luckily for Raju, a couple of days later, Rajveer was asked to go and cover for one of the three men in charge of Bali. One man had taken sick and they needed a hand building a temporary shelter for the elephant and themselves.

Raju was overjoyed. "Hurray! So, we get to come with you, then."

"Who's *we*?"

"Me and Basanti."

"No way. There's no way I'm taking you *two*."

"But why, Baba? I promise I won't cause trouble."

"When it's hard enough for me to believe that *you* won't cause trouble, I absolutely can't risk taking this langoor of yours."

Raju had struggled, but ultimately convinced Rajveer to take him to the spot where the elephant was held captive.

"Okay. Only you, though. No Basanti." Rajveer had said.

Although Raju wanted to visit the elephant eagerly, it was something he started to regret after what he saw. It didn't let him sleep that night.

They were probably a few hundred yards away from the place where the elephant was being kept when a tumultuous cry shook Raju. It certainly didn't sound human. A chill ran down his spine. As they came closer, he saw the large black-grey frame of an animal forced into a pen too small for it to fit. The elephant's rear foot had been chained to a stout wooden anchor. Thick ropes ran all over its body tying it to the wooden frame of the pen, severely restricting its movement. A man struck the animal with a rod, and it let out another shrill cry.

Raju shuddered and ran towards the animal with Rajveer trailing behind; his aged, heavy body struggling to keep up with the young lad ahead of him.

"Don't go too close, Raju," Rajveer warned. "It's a wild animal. It might hurt you."

Raju ignored him and went closer.

Standing just a few arms-lengths away from the elephant, Raju witnessed a gruelling sight. A blood-stained metal collar had warped the rear foot of the animal. Its front two legs had been tied together to a lateral wooden log – that made up one side of the pen – forcing it to stand up in a highly uncomfortable position. Raju gasped. His heart wrung with distress. He rubbed his eyes, trying to clear the image of what he was seeing, and swallowed a lump in his throat.

"Why are… Why have they tied it up?" He rummaged for words that could question the injustice done to the animal, trying to keep his voice steady at the same time.

Rajveer exchanged a few sentences with the men

in charge of the elephant. Raju just heard sounds. His eyes and mind were fixed on the animal.

"Raju. It's a wild animal. It needs to be tamed… to be calmed."

"Calmed? This way?" Raju retorted. "Who'd feel calm after being tied up in ropes?"

Rajveer softened, looking at Raju's watery eyes, and replied, "They're only following orders." He paused and lowered his aged eyes momentarily. Then said, "Major Crook's orders."

Raju looked at the Indian men and back at Rajveer. He had always disliked the Major; however, in that moment every inch of him hated the man more than ever.

"But why… How can he… Why hurt it?"

Rajveer lay a comforting hand on the child's shoulder and said, "The ways of the world are strange. They–" He broke off as if contemplating whether to tell the truth, then carried on. "They torment it to weaken the spirit of the animal… till it breaks …learns to obey…"

"Can you ask them to untie the front two feet… just this once… please?"

"But Major Crook–"

"Only for a while. Please… please… please."

"All right… all right," he said, giving in. "I'll see if I can convince these men. Just the feet, though."

Rajveer asked the men who were hesitant to go

against the Major's orders.

Raju went close to the elephant.

The elephant let out a low rumble, making Raju jump in his skin. He lay a trembling hand on the animal's flank.

"He'll be fine," Rajveer told the men. "Look, he likes the boy. The Major won't know that you untied him. You can always tie him up again if he misbehaves. But if the animal does behave, the Major will be only too pleased that you tamed him quick enough. Give it a go now. Come on."

The men looked at each other and nodded. They were simple village-men with shallow intellects, easy enough to work his words on.

Raju felt the coarse and gristly skin of the animal under his palms while the men untied the front two feet. The huge bulk of the front of the animal fell to the ground. The elephant flapped its ears and turned to Raju, as much as it could manage.

The Indian men stood back, wary and ready with their sticks to smite the animal if it misbehaved.

The elephant reached out to a small wooden branch that lay next to where Raju stood and picked it up with its trunk. The animal swung it high up in the air with its trunk and roared.

"Watch out," cried Rajveer assuming the elephant would bring it down in a fierce blow on Raju's head. He pulled Raju back.

Two men ran at the elephant, intending to strike it.

"NO. NO. STOP!" Raju screamed. "Leave him alone!"

Before the men could hit it, the elephant brought the stick down and started to etch the earth below it. It clearly had no intention of hurting anybody. But what was it up to? The men stood back, gazing ignorantly. And so did Raju and Rajveer.

A few minutes later, it flung the wooden branch away and stood shaking its trunk from side to side.

Gingerly, Raju crawled over to the spot where the elephant had carved the ground, not knowing what to expect.

Tongue-tied, he stared at the shape of a diamond – a glittering one with lines tangential to its periphery – engraved in the earth before him.

It certainly wasn't a careless, random scribble of anger and frustration. However, he didn't know what it meant... until he met Heera in the bazaar.

Chapter Seven

Raju lay awake on his bed, which was nothing more than a straw mat with a cotton sheet over it. He couldn't sleep. Rajveer's boisterous snoring didn't help, either. He shifted uncomfortably on his mat, changing sides. Nothing worked. Sleep was miles away. Even the tiniest of creaks and pops in and around the building were evident to him at this hour. The only other thing awake around him was the wall clock, ticking away, slicing the silence of the night into seconds.

He thought about the elephant and the nasty wound he had seen on its foot.

After seeing Maya, Raju had headed straight to see the elephant and to feed it bananas. Since he'd already been there, nobody would suspect him, he knew.

Earlier when Rajveer had taken him there, he had

made a mental note of the way – every little turn they had taken and every gully they had been through. First, he had to get to the Hanuman Temple which was at the outskirts of the town they lived in. That bit was the easiest. Then he had to walk North from it until he saw a cluster of trees that marked the beginning of the forest. After hitting the forest, it was about a kilometre's walk along a long and winding narrow path that looked like it had been frequently trodden by travellers, from what he remembered.

There was a rustle outside his room situated at the back of the bungalow – a part of the servants' quarters. It couldn't have been Basanti, the macaque, as she had been tied to a tree, furthest from the bungalow, behind the servants' quarters. *Perhaps the bheesti with his goat-skin bag*, Raju thought. He would come every day after dusk to sprinkle water around the bungalow to keep it cool. But it was unusually late for him to come. Probably a stray dog foraging around.

He turned on his side and looked at the wall clock in the dim light of his oil lamp. It was almost midnight and time for Benjamin's midnight snack. He sat up and stretched, then picked up his oil lamp and some carrots lying in a bowl of cold water and headed for the veranda just outside the Major's dressing room.

This part of the veranda was behind the bungalow and about fifty metres from the servants' quarters. Raju had just about set foot onto the veranda when he felt a black shadow dash past him. The darkness made it impossible to see clearly and he turned around with the oil lamp held high up in front of his face, a jitter rising through him.

There was nothing.

Raju decided his imagination was working overtime. Placing the oil lamp on the railing of the veranda, he pulled out the carrots from his pocket then opened the door to enter the Major's dressing room. The dressing room led onto the Major's bedroom, but that door was shut. In the dressing room, on a bench, sat a cage with a fluffy white rabbit.

"Here, Benjamin," Raju whispered, opening the cage and placing the carrots in front of the half-asleep animal who seemed not in the least interested in them. "Come on, eat up," he coaxed the rabbit, but it didn't budge. "I've done my job. It's up to you now. Goodnight." Raju closed the cage and tip-toed back onto the veranda. He closed the door to the dressing room gently and walked back into the darkness with the lamp in his hand lighting his way to his room.

A few steps and he froze. There was an undeniable presence behind him. A hand grabbed his torso from the back and another sealed his mouth. His eyes popped out in horror. He let go of the oil lamp. It fell down with a clatter and went out.

"Liar," a voice hissed closely into his ears. "Quiet." It was a sharp instruction; not loud but firm and livid.

"Who are you?" Raju wanted to ask, but he was gagged by the intruder's hand and too terrified to ask anyway.

He tried to pull the hand off his mouth, but the intruder's grip was strong. He struggled in vain. The hold tightened and pulled him towards the periphery of the bungalow. Raju nudged his elbow as hard as he could into the side of his captor and bit into the hand as the grip over his mouth loosened.

"Aaoouch!" The intruder stifled a shriek and let go of Raju who spun around and pushed him to the ground.

Raju was about to scream when the intruder's face caught the light of the gas lamp. He immediately recognised the tanned face, scowling and glistening with sweat. It was the boy he had met in the bazaar that very day.

"You?" Raju gasped. Relief washed over him; it was only a boy around his own age, although surprisingly strong. "Heera? Isn't that your name? How did you – you followed me, didn't you?"

"What do you think? But of course." Heera sat

up with a jerk. "Your friend – that girl – blurted out the truth. I knew from the moment I saw that drawing you made. I was certain you knew something about Bali. But you lied!" Heera's breath was coming out in short bursts. "You lied to me. A big, fat, blatant lie. I saw you – with Bali – with *my* Bali. Liar. Impostor. Why did you lie? Answer me." It was a command, not a request. Every syllable trembled with rage.

"Hush! Keep your voice down!" Raju held a finger to his lips. "We're right outside the Major's room! And you better hush up unless you want to be skinned alive."

Heera's insides sizzled with fury at the mention of the Major. He looked from the bungalow to Raju and back at the bungalow.

Raju signalled him to move further away from where they were. "Come."

He gave Heera a hand to stand up, but Heera ignored it. They crept towards the shrubbery at the side of the bungalow away from the Major's room.

"Major Crook – he lives here?" Heera whispered, his tone still incensed. "The coward – and how do I know you're not his accomplice? After all, you lied to me."

Raju nodded. "Sit down." He signed Heera to sit. "We'd better not be seen here."

Heera crouched beside Raju and held a clenched

fist to Raju's nose. "If you hadn't fed Bali, I would have straightaway knocked the daylights out of you." Raju held out his hands in front of his face trying to protect himself from an impending punch. "You're lucky I'm letting you explain yourself. Now speak up, quick. Before I change my mind."

"Hey! Take it easy. You've got it all wrong. I had nothing to do with capturing your elephant... I'm just a servant boy."

"And a busker by day," Heera added, unflinching. "Just one question. Why didn't you *tell* me about Bali? Speak."

"Look. I didn't – I would rather have told you the truth. I swear to God."

They were now sitting face to face. Heera looked at Raju's gleaming eyes. They were impish but innocent, candid but tactful, strange and yet familiar: a bundle of contradictions.

"I wanted to stay out of trouble, that's all," Raju continued. "I didn't want to draw attention to the captured elephant. I mean I didn't want to be the one drawing attention to it."

"What trouble?"

"*Any* trouble." Raju's face crumpled into unease and he unknowingly stroked his palms. They had been lashed at with the Major's cane until they bled for not polishing his shoes properly, only months ago.

"What's wrong?"

"Nothing. I meant I don't want to get in trouble with the Major. I thought if I told you and you did something stupid like try and rescue Bali or caused any distress then it might all boil down to me telling you about Bali. The Major doesn't care, probably doesn't even know, that I have visited the elephant twice now, and I would like to keep it that way. More than myself, I'm worried about getting Baba into trouble."

"Who's Baba?"

"My… my… " Raju delved for words. He hadn't thought about this before. Rajveer was everything to him. They were related by love. He hadn't put a label on the relationship before. He settled on one now and said, "My grandfather."

"And your parents… where are they?"

"I don't know… Probably dead," Raju said in a matter-of-fact way.

"I'm sorry," Heera muttered and bit his lip for asking a thoughtless question.

Think before you talk, he remembered his mother's words.

There was an awkward silence which Raju couldn't bear. He hated people feeling sorry for him. He asked a question to divert the conversation.

"So how is it that you found out it was Crook who captured the elephant?"

69

"I was there…" Heera replied, almost absent-mindedly reliving the moment. Crook's cold smile flashed before his eyes. "Only I didn't know his name, or that he is a Major, until today when Maya told me."

"The Major?" Raju asked, his eyes so wide they took up all his face. "He's seen you? This isn't good. You shouldn't be here – not anyway, but especially not since he knows your face."

"Why did you go to Bali? And how?"

"At first, Baba took me to see him. Because I insisted on it. I was excited about seeing an elephant."

Raju told Heera about the first time he saw Bali with Rajveer and how upset he was about the way the animal was being treated. Heera's fingers curled to form a fist that clenched tighter and tighter; his nails digging into the flesh on his palms. How could he have let this happen? Why hadn't he been able to protect Bali?

"You don't know Major Crook." Raju's warning cut through the tangle of thoughts in his head. "He's capable of things you can't imagine."

Heera gave a hiss of fury and banged his fist onto the ground vehemently. The piercing gravel hurt but not as much as the pain he'd been living with night and day since Bali was taken. "What does he *want*?"

"Money… that's not too difficult to predict. The

man is a greedy brute. And ruthless."

Heera recalled the sharp blow of the rifle on his head and raised his hand to touch the blue-purple bump on his forehead. It was true. The Major was a monster.

"If he wanted to, he'd have killed Bali by now. If he's trying to tame him – from what I know – then he's likely to sell him soon. He'll be loaded then. But he can't do much unless he's tamed Bali. Nobody will want to buy an elephant who will cause mayhem." Heera's eyebrows furrowed. "Didn't mean it like that," added Raju. "It's only natural for him to… for Bali… to react the way he is. The Major has been looking for a mahout ever since."

Heera remembered Bali lying on the floor, weak and hungry, when he had followed Raju to the place Bali was being kept. Ever seen flies on an animal carcass? Bali's limp body lay almost lifeless, chained to a wooden pole. Flies pestered him mercilessly and he didn't have the strength to even flicker an ear. Ruby-red blood stained the metal collar around his rear leg. Every inch of his body screamed his suffering. Heera's muscles had gone rigid with shock and pain. He couldn't cry; his throat was as dry as sawdust.

"By the way, thank you… for feeding Bali," Heera said as dryly as possible. And since it was too difficult looking at Raju while saying it, he spoke to his feet instead.

Raju clicked his tongue. Then said, "It was nothing." He plucked out a carrot from his pocket and bit into it. "Just like I feed Benjamin."

"Benjamin?" Heera peered at him. "Who's Benjamin?"

"What do you think a servant boy was doing in the bungalow at midnight? Benjamin – Crook's pet rabbit – probably was his son in the last birth – I was here to give him his midnight snack."

"What?" Heera looked at Raju utterly bewildered.

"You should go now," Raju said in a tone of increasing frustration.

Heera wondered why a rabbit needed a midnight snack. The English were crazier than he thought. But he didn't voice his surprise. All he was thinking about was how to reach Bali. And then a ridiculous thought flashed in his mind. Was it possible? Why not? he thought.

Raju had stood up, keen to end the conversation, when a light came on in the Major's room. Raju saw the Major's shadow on the curtain against the light and ducked down, immediately panicking.

"This was a bad idea. Leave. Save yourself." Raju said urgently. "Leave… Leave before he sees you here."

"I'm not scared of that coward. I want to get Bali back," Heera replied.

72

"You won't get him back by making a racket here, will you? Quite the opposite," Raju hissed. "Look, I'm going to go now. I can't be seen here with you. Get out – that side of the hedge." Raju put his palms together and looked at the sky to pray. "Save me, dear God."

But Heera wasn't perturbed. Something was cooking in his head.

"Meet me tomorrow at the Hanuman temple, before sunrise."

Raju shot a look of fury at him.

"Me? Absolutely not. I'm not meeting you – nowhere after tonight," he countered.

"You are, unless you want me here again tomorrow night. Don't be late. And get one of your shirts." And then he disappeared through the hedge as slickly as a cat.

73

Chapter Eight

Next morning, Heera woke up to the sound of stone grinding over stone. His eyes were swollen from lack of sleep. When he had finally come home it was early morning and he was welcomed by a tempest of maternal rage and worry and concern. However, Vasu didn't ask him too many questions. She was just relieved to have him back, safe and sound, and she let him catch a few hours of sleep after an initial dose of scolding.

"Where have you been, Heera? Look what you've done to yourself," Vasu grumbled on seeing him awake. "You don't eat or sleep, and you wander away aimlessly, like you did yesterday at the bazaar." She was seated with a huge stone slab between her feet with her saree drawn back up to her shins, baring her tattooed ankles. Her long, black hair was tied into a knot that sat low on her nape. She rocked to and fro, crushing chillies and onions into a fine paste, with a stout cylindrical pestle, as she spoke. "How long is this madness going to last?" Ripples ran through the geometric patterns tattooed on her wrists and upper arms as her muscles flexed and worked. The task took effort and it helped to fuel it with her vexation.

Vasu had looked for Heera at the bazaar after the monkey show had wrapped up and the crowds dispersed. But it was in vain. She had given up and gone home. Although she wasn't worried about him getting lost at that point – Heera was pretty seasoned at finding his way back home – she felt helpless thinking he had wandered away in his gloom and that she'd never have her son back, emotionally. And when he didn't come home until after midnight, she had been sick with worry and fear she had lost him for ever; even physically.

Vasu was gathering the crushed paste onto the centre of the stone slab and was about to pound it again with the stone pestle when Heera spoke. "Ma, Bali is alive."

"What?" Vasu stopped with a lump of chilli paste on her palm, to stare at Heera, sceptically. The thick skin on her palms was immune to the stinging of the chillies. "Who told you that?" It was said in a tone of disbelief, as if she was sure he'd imagined it.

"I know, Ma." He was reluctant to say anything

more.

Vasu glared at him, her light-brown eyes scorching, and slapped the paste down on the slab of stone. Some of it spattered around it.

Heera knew he had to give more detail. "I saw him."

"You did?" Vasu almost banged the pestle on the slab of stone.

"Yes, Ma. I know where they're keeping him. It's at the other end of the forest."

She stood up, pushing away a strand of stray hair with the back of her chilli-paste-coated hand, and slowly walked to Heera, her eyes enlarged in surprise, fixed on him.

"Why are you... looking at me... like that?" Heera asked, feeling his mother's penetrating stare. It was uncomfortable being looked through.

"You went there? Is that where you were last night?!" Heera looked at the floor with guilty eyes. Vasu continued with the backs of her hands on her hips, "Heera, this could be dangerous."

"But Ma, I *have* to free Bali as soon as possible."

"You're not *listening*. I said, it could be *dangerous*. How can you be so selfish?"

"Selfish? How is wanting to save my friend selfish?"

"Bali, Bali, Bali!" Vasu pivoted on her heels with her hand on her forehead. "What about me? Your mother? If something dreadful happens to you, how will I live? Have you ever thought about that? I won't be able to bear it again."

"Again?" Heera wondered.

But before he could voice his thought, Vasu spoke.

"I mean… your father." Vasu looked away.

"Mother, they'll *kill* him." He stood up jerkily, desperate to get his point across. "They're not feeding him. I can't live knowing that he's *dying* there every minute." He choked up.

Vasu walked to an earthen pot of water in the corner of the hut. She poured some into her palms and washed her hands. Wiping them on her saree, she said, "My child, come here." Sitting down next to him, she took his hand in hers and stroked his palm, pulling him closer. Cupping his face in her hands, she said, "I understand how you feel. But I can't let you hurt yourself. To the sahibs we're like insects. They'll trample us and nobody will even notice. Playing with fire will only burn you." Vasu's voice trembled with emotion. "Don't do this to yourself… and to me. You're the only one I have got. You are everything to me, my darling."

"And Bali means nothing to you, doesn't he? Just a meagre animal."

"It's not like that –"

"He may be only an animal to you but to me, he's

77

my brother." Heera interrupted. He shrugged away her arms and stood to get away from her. "He's my friend. I can't watch him die and live on knowing I could have done something about it. That I could have tried at the very least."

"But it could mean putting yourself at risk!"

"It well could be. But it's better than living with guilt, eating away at me my whole life."

"Sometimes you have to let go of what you love dearly... even if it's excruciatingly painful." Her eyes wandered away, distant and detached. "Because you can't lose what you already have. We have each other, don't we?"

Heera rolled his eyes. His mother would never understand, he decided. There was an ocean between them, and his words – no matter how many – just couldn't reach her.

And then Heera remembered. It was dawn, the sun was rising, and he had to be at the Hanuman temple. Without thinking or saying any more, he ran out.

"Come back, Heera," Vasu cried to no avail. "Where are you going now?" But Heera didn't stop. Vasu drew her knees up and hugged them to her chest and sobbed.

Chapter Nine

Heera waited with bated breath behind the Hanuman temple, just outside its back wall. The sun had almost risen. Was he late? He watched men and women rush by with baskets of marigold and incense sticks and sweets, eager to worship Bajrang Bali (after whom Heera had named Bali) early in the morning. His tangerine-coloured idol stood tall in the middle of the temple. The Hindu priests chanted Sanskrit mantras and devotees sang praises of the lord. The whole place reeked of the pungent, musky smell of the marigolds and the piquant scent of camphor.

It was soon late morning and the sun had fully risen. Heera was tired of waiting. He had already eaten a few java plums he'd found at home. He pulled out a guava, sat down on his haunches and sank his teeth into the fruit. If Raju didn't come before he finished the fruit, he would leave, he decided. He picked out a few seeds from in between his teeth and spat them out. Dejected, he ate the last piece of fruit and stood up to go when he saw a figure appear at the corner of the temple. Heera smiled in his mind but tried not to look too pleased. It was Raju.

"I knew you'd come," he said when Raju was close enough to hear.

"What do you *want* from me?" He threw the shirt he'd brought along at Heera. "Apart from this?"

"I need your help."

"I told you yesterday that I can't help and risk myself and Baba."

"I want to come and meet the Major at his bungalow."

"You what?" Raju was baffled. "Are you mental? Why would you want to walk to your own grave — no — I mean — are you serious?"

"Listen." Heera wrapped his palm around the fist he made with his other hand and squeezed it. "There's something I've come up with — a plan — and for that I need to see him."

"I don't know what to say." Raju shrugged.

"He won't recognise me. You'll be surprised how invisible people in tattered, dirty clothes are." Raju still looked puzzled. So Heera explained, "My whole body and face were coated in a paste of mud from falling into a mud pit before I reached him that day in the forest – the day Bali was caught. This time, it'll be a cleaner version of me. That'll be my disguise. I'm going to offer my services as a mahout to Bali." Heera looked away from Raju to hide the longing in his eyes that poured out without warning at the thought of Bali. "I can't think of any other way to get near him."

"What if he says no?" Raju asked.

"I don't know…" Heera looked at him, annoyed. It was the last thing he wanted to think of. Failure. "Why would he say no to someone who can help him achieve what he wants? A calm and trained elephant. I can demonstrate it to the Major. Once he sees how calm and comfortable Bali is with me – which he will be without doubt – he will trust me. That's my only chance to reach out to Bali and then I can work out how to set him free. I'll worry about that later."

"Later? When? After you're killed?" Raju spat. "That's your plan?" Raju raised his eyebrows disapprovingly.

"It'll work. I'll come up with something. You'll see."

"Fine, what can I do?" Raju realised there was no point trying to persuade Heera.

"The Major. I think he'll be convinced if someone – if your Baba – can recommend me as a mahout. I don't speak English. It will help to have

81

your Baba around anyway. He knows a bit of English, doesn't he?"

"A recommendation? Look, keep me and Baba out of this. We're not getting involved in this *plan* of yours."

Heera started to bite his nails. Was his plan already falling apart? He'd never felt so dependent on someone else. And just when he had begun to wonder if he had made a mistake by making his intentions known to someone who didn't want to help, Raju spoke.

"I won't give you away, though. So don't worry about that. But that doesn't mean I'm helping. If you're caught – which is most likely to happen – I don't know you and you don't know me. We've never seen each other. Get it? And Baba isn't recommending nobody. I don't–"

"When will I find Crook at the bungalow?" Heera asked, cutting through Raju's jabbering. "Tomorrow?"

"Uh… You don't listen well, do you?"

Heera nodded trying to summon up confidence. "I'll see him anyway. I don't need anybody recommending me," he said firmly. "Tomorrow?" Heera stressed his question.

"Well… yes. Actually… there's a party tomorrow evening."

"A party?"

"Yes, lots of guests, food and drink, more than an elephant can eat." Raju smirked.

"I'll be there then."

"You're coming to the party?"

"Do you think I'm invited?" He smiled. "Just want to meet the Major."

There was a brief patch of silence until Raju spoke again.

"I don't know… up to you really. Only make sure he doesn't recognise you, else–" Raju raised his outstretched palm and ran it in front of his neck like a blade slicing it. "–you're dead." He rolled his eyes back like a dead man's. "Can ask Maya to give you her kajal…" He winked. "…if you like."

Maya. Heera thought of the girl he had met in the bazaar.

You don't recognise me, do you? Her voice resounded in his ears.

"That girl… I know her," Heera mumbled under his breath, more to himself.

"Did you say something?"

Heera shook his head. "Nothing."

Raju nodded and then bid him goodbye.

Heera waved absent-mindedly, trying to figure out what Maya had meant. And then it came to him…

Chapter Ten

About a year earlier...

Heera was in the forest plucking mangoes when a muffled cry from somewhere behind him made him jump. Startled, he looked around. Then he climbed down the tree and started to walk in the direction he thought the cry had come from. There was a crunching sound in the dry leaves on the forest floor not far from where he was. He carried on walking towards an area of dense undergrowth, unable to see through it, cutting through it with his scythe.

Heera almost always carried his scythe with him into the forest. It was a handy tool to cut through the undergrowth, and also a weapon of self-defence against predators like cheetahs and tigers, although these animals were not likely to attack unless frightened. However, the forest was full of surprises.

The light was feeble as the late-afternoon sun could only filter through the occasional gaps between trees.

A low growling came. And then it stopped abruptly. Something near him had sensed his presence. He wasn't alone. A shiver danced down his spine. Whoever or whatever it was, was not very far away. It was just behind the huge trunk of the tree in front of him. He knew; it was intuition. There was no rational explanation for it.

Heera held the scythe before him, ready to attack. A gasp sounded. He slashed forward through the dense foliage towards the tree and immediately regretted doing so. His eyes grew as big as plates.

He saw the back of a girl. She sat on her haunches, stupefied, eye-to-eye with a black cobra a few feet from her. The snake stood as tall as a third of its body length, jerking its extended hood forward whilst emitting a low-pitched hiss. Or was it more like a growl? This is what he had heard through the bushes moments ago. Heera had disturbed it more than it already was. Its bifid tongue sprang out.

The girl winced, trying hard not to cry. The forest breeze rustled through her untied waist-length hair, blowing tendrils of it around, some sticking to her upper lip speckled with sweat.

"Don't move," whispered Heera. "Don't *move*." Heera knew that snakes, particularly cobras, hated movement. And he'd just violated the rule himself.

Sweat trickled from the girl's forehead. She

fought her nerves to sit still.

Heera took a gentle step forward, watching the snake. And then another. The snake didn't take any heed of Heera.

"Stay still… calm… *breathe*." He spoke slowly and in a whisper. Clearly it wasn't working. The girl was now shaking.

Heera had to do something. Keeping his eyes on the cobra, he walked in a circle, every step measured, approaching the snake from behind. The U-shape on its hood revealed itself from a few feet away. His heart gave a jolt with the realisation. It was a spitting cobra.

To avoid making a sound, he gestured to the girl, who was now in front of him, to close her eyes. And as soon as she did, Heera seized the snake's tail and lifted it upward. In a flash the cobra spat out its venom which spattered across the girl's arm. She shrieked in horror and leapt to her feet. The cobra squirmed in mid-air, dangling loose from its tail grasped in Heera's grip.

Keeping an eye on the snake, Heera put a finger to his lips and threw the girl a glance. "Stop yelling." His tone was steady and firm. "You're making it nervous. It's harmless on your skin – the venom. *Wipe* it off."

The girl fell silent. Holding her arm out stiff and away from her body, she turned around to find some leaves. Venom dribbled down her skin.

Heera bent down till the cobra touched the ground, its hood and the upper half of its body writhing edgily below. *It's a female.*

"I won't harm you," he said to the snake. His voice was sombre but soft. "But you better be a good girl."

Glancing at the tree behind the girl, he spoke softly again, not wanting to agitate the cobra. "Move away from the tree. She thinks you're a threat. There's a nest there – most likely – with eggs in it."

The girl who was now busy wiping the venom off her arm with a few green leaves, shifted away from the tree.

With the blunt back of his scythe, Heera pushed down on the hood of the cobra, firmly but gently. "Easy. Easy," he comforted the snake. The cobra eased its hood down for a moment and stretched out on the ground to its full length before raising its hood back up towards Heera who was still holding its tail.

The girl gasped with awe and terror at the nine-foot snake.

Heera bent slightly, still holding the tail a few feet above the ground. He looked at the cobra with a placidity that was incomprehensible to the girl. Cupping his other hand into a hood-like shape, he swivelled his cupped hand around his wrist a couple of times in a direction away from him, trying to direct the snake away.

The girl watched astounded.

The cobra followed Heera's hand and turned in the direction that Heera was willing it to go. Then easing its hood, it wriggled on the ground. Heera smiled and released its tail.

Good girl! he thought.

The cobra slithered away.

Heera straightened his back and smiled briefly at the girl, looking away instantly.

The girl stood stony still, shocked to the bone.

"Are you all right?" he asked, looking in the direction the snake had slithered away.

"Y-yes. Thank you," the girl mumbled back, holding on shakily to the sides of her ankle-length skirt.

She was about the same age as Heera and wore a short blouse – exposing a few inches of her tawny midriff – in the same shade of forest-green as her skirt, making her blend with the surroundings.

"The worst thing you can do when confronted by a snake is to scream or move. It can mean the difference between life and death. Remember that." The girl wobbled her head from side to side in an Indian nod.

"You're… brave," she said, trying to find her voice.

Heera looked away, awkward with the compliment.

"What's your name?" He diverted the conversation.

"Maya."

He nodded. "The venom is harmless on your skin. But not in your eyes. Even a drop can blind you in minutes. That's why I asked you to shut them, in case some of it were to splash into your eyes. Never mind–" he looked around. "What were you doing here? How did you find yourself with a cobra?"

"I come to the forest sometimes to peel cinnamon bark, with my father," she said, relaxing a little, wiping the sweat off her brow with the back of her upper arm. "This part of the forest has many cinnamon trees."

"But where *is* your father?"

"Somewhere there – not far… hopefully." She pointed to the east. "Appa has a fruit shop but also sells cinnamon bark to the merchants."

Heera looked at the tree. It wasn't a cinnamon tree but a jamun tree.

As if reading his mind, the girl said. "Erm… I wandered away looking for jamuns. And when I found the tree, I climbed up to pick some. When I jumped down–"

"Ah! You must have disturbed its nest," Heera interrupted. "Look." He nodded in the direction of the tree. "It's just there, at the foot of the tree. See that cluster of dry leaf litter? That's the nest…" Maya looked at the nest and back at Heera. "Anyways, I think you should go back now," Heera said, looking in the direction she had pointed to. "To your father. He'll be worried."

"The way you handled that cobra!" Maya's voice was full of astonishment.

"Nothing really… They're not aggressive creatures." Heera dropped his head, busying himself with the leaves underfoot, tossing them around with his toe, ears burning.

"Really? After all that hissing and venom-spitting!"

"They aren't. That's self-defence." Heera looked up, voice tight. He couldn't bear someone falsely accusing a speechless reptile. "They can sense your chemistry. If they sense fear, they see you as a threat. Moreover, you were very close to her nest. That snake was a female. They can get hostile defending their eggs. It's maternal instinct. All creatures have it. That's how nature made them." He sounded like the snake's advocate.

"Okay. I get it." Maya knew she couldn't win. "But how do you know so much about snakes?"

"Ma… she taught me," Heera replied shortly, keen to wrap up the conversation. He wasn't the kind of person who'd blow his own trumpet.

"Anyone can learn, really." He shrugged.

"How did *she* know?"

"She was raised in her tribe and taught young. An expert snake-catcher ever since she was as old as me… I think."

"Wow! That sounds exciting. And who taught her?"

This wasn't ending. The girl had a question for every answer that came out of his mouth. Heera mentally scoffed. Although, he didn't want to be rude to her.

"Her father, a skilled snake-catcher, was also a herbalist. He caught snakes to extract their venom and used it in herbal medicines. He taught her." He glimpsed at the sun above. It had started to set, making the light fade around them. "Anyways, I should get going now. It's not safe here when you can't see much. You should go back too. Your father may be looking–"

Maya again wobbled her head from side to side, to say yes, although unenthusiastically.

Perfectly timed, there was a muffled call from somewhere behind them. "Maya. Maya."

"It must be Appa." Maya turned to look. "Coming, Appa. I'm coming."

When she turned back to look at Heera, he had already dashed a considerable distance away.

"Thank you…" she cried cupping her hands

91

around her mouth. "…for saving my life."
He ran unheeding, her voice diminishing.

Chapter Eleven

Heera woke up earlier than usual. He stood outside the hut and stretched his arms high above his head, admiring the beautiful morning alive with bird song and the blue-grey sky which was cracking in places to allow the hues of orange and pink through. He wondered how Bali was doing at that very moment, then closed his eyes and shrugged the thought away. There was not much time to waste. It was the time to stay focussed and act. Vasu was away collecting wood in the forest, and he had woken up early to take advantage of her absence.

Quickly he searched the hut for a little metal box that held kajal which Vasu used to highlight her eyes, but he couldn't find it. He didn't want to ask her for it either and arouse her suspicion. So he decided to make it himself, like he'd seen his mother do before.

Pouring some ghee his mother had made few days ago into a small diya, he dipped a cotton wick in it to soak up the fat and lit it. Holding a shallow earthen bowl on top of the fire, he let the silky black smoke coat the inside of the bowl with soot. Scraping the feathery, fine powder off the bowl carefully, he mixed it with a few drops of ghee adding only a drop at a time, just like his mother did, careful not to make it too runny. He was pleased with the viscous, homogeneous, black paste he had made; organic kajal.

Next, he flung open a trunk that lay deserted in the corner of the hut, setting off a mushrooming cloud of dust over it. In it, there were a couple of his old clothes that he had outgrown. And a few from when he was a baby. He wondered why his mother kept them still. From underneath these garments, peeked a brilliant shade of vermillion. A saree.

Although the saree belonged to Vasu, Heera didn't remember his mother ever wearing it. Not even in his earliest memories. After all, she was a widow, forbidden to wear any colour apart from white or cream or beige. That's how he'd always seen her; his father had died of cholera when he was only a toddler.

When he was much younger, Heera had, at times, seen his mother stroking the saree discreetly before putting it back without uttering a word. That memory reminded him of the ache in his mother's eyes. He had hated the saree in his early years, thinking it had made her miserable. It wasn't until a few years ago that he realised it wasn't the saree but the loss of his father that caused her the misery.

Heera heaved a sigh and pulled the saree out from beneath the pile of clothes, lifting it up to admire the golden border that ran all along its length. He nestled his face into it and let his cheek feel the silky caress of the garment. It smelled new, dusty and ancient, all at the same time. But most of all, it smelled like Mother.

A piece of it would make a perfect turban. Striking and rich. That's how he could look presentable enough to meet the Major. As far as possible, he had to try and look unlike the boy Crook had seen in the forest, defending his elephant; a nobody.

Sorry Ma. I'll stitch it back, I promise.

The silky folds glided over themselves slipping from Heera's hold and the saree unfurled carelessly. Something rolled out of the folds of fabric and fell to his feet with a clink. Heera's eyes darted to the object and widened. His jaw fell open.

He picked up the object with quivering hands. It was familiar to him… from his dreams.

The tiny silver anklet shone in the dull morning

light. It was as thick as a child's little finger, barely enough to round a small apple and smooth and round all over except in one place where two ball-like shapes touched each other. The shapes weren't welded together. They could be parted for the anklet to be worn.

Heera couldn't believe his eyes. It was exactly like the one that sat on the ankle of the crying child.

A million questions hit his mind like a raging hurricane.

How come Mother had this anklet? Why had she never mentioned it to him despite knowing about his dreams? Was she keeping something from him? And why?

Looking at it closely, he could see a few words engraved on it. Heera couldn't read but he could tell it was in Hindi. He ran his fingers over the carvings as if feeling them would reveal the meaning of the words. Finally, he memorised the words like a drawing. After all, they were merely shapes and patterns to him.

Why hadn't Mother ever mentioned it? The thought pestered him. He pushed the thought away. There was a lot to get done before Mother came back.

With a knife, he managed to cut a sizeable piece out of the saree and folded the rest as neatly as he could, hiding the untidy zigzag end that had suffered the cut, so that it looked like it had never been touched. He tucked the anklet inside the folds of the saree. He'd get back to it later, he decided.

Heera then took a piece of sandalwood and sat down on his haunches to grind it on the stone slab. He dribbled a few drops of water over the wood and started to rub it against the coarse surface feeling its powdery, creamy touch as the wood dissolved into the water releasing its piney, warm, and sweet aroma. Heera collected the fragrant paste and folded it gently inside a piece of banana leaf.

He then scurried outside the hut with his precious acquisition and creations and put them under a tree that stood at the back of the hut and covered them with a jute sack. A green keelback snake slithered by, over the roots of the tree. It flattened its neck and raised its head like a cobra, sensing Heera.

"Oh! Hello there," Heera said softly, crouching down in front of the snake. "Calm down. How would I know you were basking in the sunshine here?"

The snake didn't budge, maintaining its hood.

"Now don't give me false threats. We both know there's nothing in your fangs... I didn't mean any harm." Heera smiled, admiring the colours on the snake's body.

It had an inverted black V-mark on the neck, its apex forwards, reaching to the frontal shield, and a second much smaller one behind. Its yellow-green head and moderately large green eyes glinted in the early morning sun. The snake sank down, its hood diminished, and it slowly slithered over and across Heera's foot while he sat unflinching.

Heera then heard his mother at the front of the hut and peeked from the side. Vasu staggered towards the hut with a bundle of wood on her head.

On cue, Heera snapped off the twig of the neem tree not far from him and started to chew on it. The bitter tang of the neem was jarring to the insides of his mouth. It was unpleasant; the bitterest of bitter he had ever known. And he had to be nagged to do so every day.

"Ah... Look who's up." Vasu spoke, gasping for air. She beamed and put the bundle of wood down. "And brushing already?!" She paused with her hands on her hips to look at her son curiously. Her chest rose and fell rapidly from the exhaustion of carrying the weight.

Heera carried on casually then spat out the slimy bitter mixture that had formed in his mouth and wiped his lips on the back of his arm.

"That's like my good boy," Vasu said wiping the sweat off her forehead with the end of her saree.

Later that afternoon, when Vasu left for the bazaar to sell wood, Heera washed his face, moistened his fingers with water and spit and ran them through his short hair to make it look as neat as possible. He struggled but lined his eyes with the kajal like he had seen his mother do. They looked messy but the smudges weren't that evident on his brown skin. After he had put Raju's shirt on, he carefully stuck his thumb into the sandalwood paste and rounded a cooling, fragrant spot between his eyebrows. The last task was by far the hardest. After a few attempts he had something that resembled a turban on his head.

Heera looked at the pentagonal piece of mirror implanted in the mud wall. Its bare boundaries reminded him of the day his fears had come alive and prevented him from embellishing its periphery. The day Bali had been captured.

He looked into the mirror anyway. A well-groomed and astonished village boy blinked back. He looked striking.

Chapter Twelve

Nervous but resolute, Heera sat in a tree yards away from the main gate of the Major's bungalow, waiting for the daylight to diminish. It gave him a good view of where he was about to go.

A moderately high hedge bordered the bungalow and hid a sprawling lawn behind it. And to the right of the lawn was a driveway, paved with stone, running from the gate to the main door of the bungalow. A row of Ashoka trees lined the driveway, separating it from the lawn, each of them up-lit by gas-lamps. The effect was spectacular; something Heera had never seen. Light to him came from a fire. Nothing more. Nothing less. This was a lavish display of money, position, and power.

A stout chowkidar sat in uniform at the front gate, with a lantern in his hand, chewing on betelnut like a masticating cow.

Heera climbed down the tree. He set his jaw and marched ahead with the audacity of a soldier in a war zone.

The chowkidar looked at him as if he'd spotted an ant.

"Oi! Who're you?" he asked, scanning Heera from top to toe.

"I would like to meet Major Sahib," Heera said firmly but respectfully.

"Major sahib?" The watchman sneered. "Who is he? Your uncle?"

"Erm – No." Heera thought it was a dumb reply, but it had already slipped out. Wrestling his mind to keep his nerves at bay he said, "I want to see him. It's important."

"*Want* to?" The chowkidar mocked. "And I want to drink all the expensive wine being served inside." He chortled. Then said scornfully, "That's not how it works. There's a party going on with *very important* people in it. And nothing about you looks important. Get lost."

Heera turned, tightening his fists to contain the fury arising within him, and started to walk away while the watchman rambled on. "Where do these lunatics come from?"

Heera noticed a place in the hedge on the left side of the bungalow that had thinned out. It was quite sparse in one spot whilst the rest of it was dense and green. Making sure he wasn't noticed by the watchman, he slid to the side of the bungalow and managed to squeeze his thin frame through the hedge, emerging onto a manicured lawn on the other side behind a row of red crotons that ran in a straight line parallel to the hedge. To his left was the bungalow and on his right in the corner of the garden was a rocky fountain with water gushing out of the mouths of two huge marble fish.

A wave of drunken laughter erupted from inside. He peeked from behind the plants to look at the bungalow. A rush of giggles, music and natter, and the clinking of glasses followed. The smell of grilled meat and spices made his mouth water and his stomach roar. It was a world he had never visited; absolutely alien.

He brushed the leaves out of his turban that had come loose, and dusted his shirt, still crouching low behind the crotons. Then he crept to the fountain behind the cluster of rocks to wash his hands. After he'd had a drink to cool his insides, he undid his turban and tied it again, so that it looked neat, checking his appearance in the rippling pond water. And he stopped. Once the ripples had disappeared, he saw himself reflected back, a scrawny boy in an outfit that didn't even belong to him. He looked conspicuous. A striking contrast to the people inside. Talk about a sore thumb. He felt utterly stupid. The chowkidar was right. What had he been thinking? Why would the Major even bother looking at him, let alone speak to him?

However, since he had come so far, he thought it better to explore. Staying low behind the crotons he crept to the end of the row of plants towards the left, onto the veranda at the side of the bungalow. The daylight had faded and darkness was taking over. There was a dark patch, near a window, which had escaped any lighting while most of the bungalow was lit. His heart thudded as he peeked in from the window to take a look inside. He gawked.

Men and women, dressed in suits and hats and gowns and satin and silk, stood with glasses in their hands, some chattering, some laughing, some blowing out plumes of smoke and some so drunk they could barely stand. The room was lined with oak wood panels. Ivory ornaments and stuffed animal heads sat proudly in every corner of the room. The furniture was all solid wood. And the place reeked of smoke, alcohol, and meat. An entourage of servants went back and forth with trays of food and wine, offering it to the guests and clearing away used plates.

"Get out, you moron!" bellowed a man who appeared right in front of the window Heera was looking through.

Heera ducked immediately and froze. His heart

cartwheeled. Had he been caught? A clamour of trays and cutlery crashing followed.

"But, Sir… It was–" came the quivering plea of a man who spoke English with a heavy Indian accent. And before he could even complete his sentence, the man gave out a miserable wail.

"Buffoon! Shut up. Don't you have the sense to know what needs to be kept and what doesn't?"

Shaken, Heera peeked through the window with just one eye to see the back of an English man in a suit. The gentleman's thick golden-brown hair was slicked back with gel. Clearly, the man was brimming with rage. A tanned Indian servant lay on the floor clutching his abdomen as if he'd been kicked in it. Hard. Heera ignored the tug of sympathy at his heart, knowing he couldn't do much.

"How *dare* you hurt Benjamin's feelings, you clumsy oaf!" Spittle few out of the Englishman's mouth. He shook with the intensity of his wrath, unable to maintain the volume of his shouting.

The room full of people watched, frozen. All eyes were glued to the scene.

Heera watched horrified. None of the words uttered made any sense to him although the name Benjamin, rang a bell. He certainly knew that name.

And, coincident with his moment of realisation, came another sentence spitting out, as livid as all the ones uttered already by the Englishman, if not more so. "How *dare* you serve rabbit meat? Can't you see how – how would Benjamin feel about seeing others of his own fraternity served on a plate?"

The guests in the room who had a piece of the rabbit meat and were about to bite into it, put it away immediately.

Heera wondered what was wrong with the food that had made the man so angry.

The meat was strewn across the floor in an ugly muddle. A couple of servants rushed to the site. Some began clearing up the mess and ran back to get more staff to help the groaning Indian man servant up. As they walked out, Heera heard a few voices in Hindi speak amongst themselves.

"Sahib is very upset."

"Who'd have imagined serving rabbit meat would have angered him so much."

"You know how he is – crazy about Benjamin."

"If only I'd known what was on the menu. Poor Shyam. He's hurt badly."

"Let's get him out of there quickly before he's killed."

What Raju had said about Benjamin and his midnight snack now suddenly made sense to Heera. The realisation of who must be standing with his back to the window he was looking through hit him like a bucket of ice-cold water. Warily he peeked back in.

The Englishman spun around to look at one of the servants standing next to him. And Heera instantly recognised the smug face and vicious eyes from the howdah on top of the elephant in the jungle when Bali was being captured. *The Major.*

The Major's right eye twitched severely – just like it had done when Heera had seen him for the very first time. Heera gasped with his mouth hanging open. Air went in and out, but he didn't make a sound.

"Useless country-bumpkin," the Major yelled, thrusting his leather-shod foot into the back of the servant still lying on the floor and already recoiling in pain. The servant squealed in agony. Heera flinched. "You're lucky I don't have you skinned alive. Take him away."

Soon the groaning man was carried away by a few Indian staff.

The Major tugged at the royal blue silk scarf around his neck, uneasily. All the fuming had caused him to sweat, gluing the silk to his skin. A plume of hair had fallen out of place, onto his forehead.

Heera sat down under the window, in a daze.

The man was insane, he decided. Deranged. Absurd. A maniac. Heera was now rethinking his plan. Was there any point meeting the Major, when he was in such a mood? Probably not. Absolutely not, he decided.

"Some chicken and lamb on skewers. *Quick!*" The Major spat instructions at the servants who flew out of the room as fast as their legs could carry them to execute the command. He slicked his hair back in place, brazen-faced, and reached for his box of cigars to pull one out. "Sorry about the disruption, ladies and gentlemen," he said, forcing a smile that betrayed all innocence, and swaying the cigar between his fingers. "We'll have some more food out soon. In the meantime, drink and be merry!"

The crowd returned to their drinks and conversations almost instantly as if nothing had happened.

Major Crook held the cigar in his mouth.

Heera wondered what that thick and stumpy thing was. He had seen the village folk smoke bidis before but those were made out of leaves and much thinner. The cigar looked ten times thicker.

Crook pulled out a small device from his coat pocket. He spun his thumb on it and a flame jerked out which he lit his cigar with. He blew a huge plume of smoke, creating a cloud in front of his face that rose above his head.

Heera watched with awe at the ease and effortlessness with which fire had been made. He had never seen a lighter before, or even a cigar. The only way he knew to make a fire was by striking stones or wood together – a work of art and patience. And even though he was an expert at it, it had taken him years of practice to learn. On the other hand, this looked as easy as batting an eyelid.

The Major turned without looking directly at the window and placed the lighter on the window sill. For a moment Heera cringed and jolted back into the shadows.

There was too much to take in. How could somebody who was so abnormally sensitive about his pet want to harm another animal? The Major was a paradox. An utter contradiction.

The thought lingered for a second and then the contradiction screamed out to him. He could use it. He allowed himself a small smile. And waited until it was midnight.

Chapter Thirteen

The door on the veranda at the back of the bungalow creaked open. A little figure with a lantern stepped out. It was Raju with Benjamin's midnight snack. Heera watched intently from the shrubbery. He could see the servants' quarters further down to the right of the kitchen. And close to where he sat stood a six-foot high stack of dung cakes. That was the only part of the bungalow's surroundings that smelt like home.

The whole place was still buzzing with people. Servants rushed back and forth between the kitchen and the bungalow. Heera had been sitting tight for hours in a small dark corner in the shrubbery, near the kitchen, hoping for the party to end and for traffic in and around the bungalow to recede. His legs had gone numb; they tingled from keeping so still. Every minute stretched out like an age. He had waited and waited for the right moment to act on his plan.

The plan was to kidnap Benjamin.

He had to seize the trump card; else he stood no chance of getting Bali back.

He probably would have to come back again in a few days, Heera thought, when he noticed one of the Indian servants walk towards him. He stiffened with fear at the sound of the approaching footsteps and stooped lower into the bushes for cover, closing his eyes. The man halted a few feet from the shrubs and looked around to make sure he wasn't being seen. Then he took a bidi out of his pocket and lit it. Heera didn't care to look until he was done. No sooner had the man let out a satisfying sigh and a cloud of smoke, than a voice shouted out his name.

"Ramlal... take this to the bungalow. NOW!"

Heera peeked through the corner of his eye. With a jerk, the man threw his bidi to the floor, swore and put it out with his shoes.

"Coming," he shouted back, trying to hide his aggression, and scurried in the direction of the kitchen. Something came tumbling out of his pocket and fell to the ground, but he walked away, unaware.

Heera heaved a sigh of relief watching the man leave. And then he squinted at the little silver object glinting in the scanty light a few feet from where he

110

sat. With a small stick he broke off the shrubbery, he managed to draw it towards him without exposing himself. The object was small, long, and rectangular and had a wheel at the top on one side. He had seen the Major use something like this just moments ago. He knew it made fire.

Heera held it with the marvel of a toddler who had discovered ice. He spun his thumb at the wheel like he'd seen the Major do and lurched in joy when the flame lit. He admired it, cross-eyed. It was precious. But the lighter wasn't his to keep. He wasn't a thief. The excitement faded as fast as it had dawned. And then it came rushing back again with a thought that hit him like lightning. He couldn't keep it, but he could borrow it. To achieve what he had been sitting there for. And borrowing wasn't stealing.

All he had to do was to create a distraction at the front of the bungalow. And what better distraction could there be than a fire. It was sure to draw everyone to the front. Moreover, there was a pond and fountain in the garden and a hose lying there too which he'd seen earlier. That, he hoped, would make the most logical choice to extinguish the fire and keep everyone busy enough and out at the front, to give him the time to take Benjamin away from the back of the bungalow. He knew which door on the back veranda led to Benjamin. He'd seen Raju go through it earlier.

Heera looked around and quickly scrambled behind the pile of dung cakes. He untied his turban and placed it on the ground. Then carefully and slowly he picked a few dung cakes from the back of the pile, making sure it didn't collapse, as that would draw attention to him. Holding more than a dozen dung cakes, secured close with a knot in the turban he scrambled back along the shrubbery to the front of the bungalow. He could see the chowkidar across at the gate, practically dozing off. There were a few motor cars now parked on the driveway in single file. One of them was practically touching the bushes. Heera had always wondered how these huge boxes moved on four wheels. He had seen only a few around.

Lying down to look under it, he checked for any feet around. There was nobody in the vicinity. He slipped out the dung cakes and slid them under the vehicle. Then he flicked the lighter on and took a deep breath and lit the little heap under the car. Rapidly he scrambled back and tied the piece of turban cloth around his waist.

The dung cakes took to fire almost immediately, and Heera scampered away as soon as he could to get out of there before it attracted people. Ducking behind the shrubbery, he ran low to where he had been sitting and waited, crossing his fingers, hands, and legs.

112

Nothing happened. Not even a scream. Had the fire gone out? Had his plan flopped before it even started? And then it came. A distant shriek from the front of the bungalow, loud enough to be heard.

"Fire! Fire! The car is on fire! Water! Get water!"

At first, it was just one person shouting in Hindi. Must have been the watchman or one of the chauffeurs or staff. Then a couple of others joined in.

Heera smiled. Looked like his plan would work after all. Although this was only the start.

An earth-shaking BOOM and BANG followed. The car had exploded into flames. Heera's heart galloped in his chest like a wild stallion. What had happened? He hadn't seen this coming. This sounded like a multitude of gunshots going off together.

One of the English guests started to shout out for help. The shrieking was contagious and it went wild like a forest fire. In no time there was a tumultuous uproar of people yelling and panicking; voices ramming into each other. There was no distinction of language anymore. Only panic. Pure, thick, intense panic. Almost tangible.

A river of people poured out of the servants' quarters and the kitchen like a swarm of honey bees on a mission. There was chaos inside the bungalow too. The servants rushed to the front of the

113

bungalow, some carrying pots and pans and pails of water. Heera watched unmoving. His heart skipped a beat. He feared people were going to run back and forth for water which wouldn't give him the time to reach Benjamin and sneak away with him.

Soon, a huge crowd had gathered to the front of the bungalow. The backyard was practically empty now. Every servant there had just one motive: to put out the fire while the guests stood at a safe distance and gasped.

Heera could hear splashes of water. The servants had been scooping water out of the pond with whatever they had – buckets, saucepans, pots – and throwing it over the flames.

This was Heera's chance. He had to act fast. Covering his face with the piece of vermillion cloth around his waist, to leave only his eyes uncovered, Heera checked the ground was clear. He crept to the back veranda and flicked off the two oil lanterns there to make his presence inconspicuous. With senses as sharp as his, darkness had never been an enemy. A pallid shaft of moonlight the only illumination there was, Heera's pupils dilated to take in all the light. Tiptoeing to the door, he grabbed the handle, unbolted it and slipped inside.

A waft of musky, woody cologne hit him. The lights were off. He stepped in and closed the door behind him. Then he flicked the lighter on. To his left was a stand that held hats and coats. And behind it was a wardrobe, although it looked alien to Heera who had only ever owned one piece of clothing, let alone a wardrobe full of clothes.

The flame licked the metal plate and singed his finger. Heera let go and the flame went out. To his right, there was a shuffle in the dark. He turned and walked towards the outline of a cage. A white ball of fluff moved slightly inside it – glowing in whatever light it caught – standing out in the darkness around it. Heera flicked the lighter on again. And stood gawking.

Glowing in the orange light of the fire was a cage made of gold. It was huge, almost four feet wide and deep and tall – ornate and royal. The inside of the cage was lined with purple velvet that was quilted to make a springy mattress for Benjamin who sat innocently nibbling on a carrot, oblivious to the luxuries around him. Rabbit pellets covered most of the velvet, leaving it smelly. A fluffy pillow covered in velvet and lace trimmings lay in a corner of the cage. Its corners had been nibbled at. The extravagance almost knocked Heera off his feet. He cupped his mouth with his hand. This rabbit was *special* to the Major.

A sadness tugged at his heart. He felt sorry for Benjamin; after all a cage was a cage no matter what it was made of and whatever luxury it had in it. It still was a slayer of freedom.

Heera shook himself out of the jumble of wonder and angst. He put the lighter out and dropped it to the floor and, without further ado, took Benjamin out of the cage. Then he opened the door onto the veranda and sneaked out with the rabbit into the darkness.

Chapter Fourteen

Vasu was mad at Heera and worried sick as usual when he returned early in the morning. But she fell silent on seeing Benjamin in Heera's arms. At first, she was curious but soon relieved. Her son had a new pet; or that is what she thought. Nothing mattered as long as he looked happy and she didn't probe any further. Neither did Heera bother explaining himself. He had, however, wiped the kajal clean off his eyes with coconut oil and hidden the piece of vermillion cloth which was a part of Vasu's saree inside his shirt, to avoid his mother's questions.

At the bungalow, Major Crook had turned a wild and fiery shade of red. The servants were told to line up in single file. They stood, heads hanging, quivering like leaves while he prowled the entire row like a tiger who would at any second bite someone's head off.

"What in the *world* happened last night?" The Major spoke with a stormy intensity and a severe scowl. "First rabbit meat to *ruin* my party – then my car on *fire* – next Benjamin!" The Major threw his hands up in rage. "He's gone! From *under* your noses. Just like that!" He clicked his fingers. "Or is one of you a part of this?" He stopped to peer at a few faces that hung with their eyes glued to the ground, gulping back their nerves. "I'll have each of you thrown out if I don't get him back." The Major quaked with every word and spittle flew out of his mouth. His right eye twitched wildly. "Move your backsides, you clumsy oafs. Now out!"

Later that morning, Heera created an enclosure with a wooden fence and bound straw mats to it, to release Benjamin into. He didn't want the rabbit jumping out and escaping; however, he also wanted the animal to have a sizeable area to itself. He worked with a sense of purpose and handled Benjamin with the same care and respect he had for other forms of life in the forest.

Vasu left him alone. This was better than seeing him lost and grave.

Heera didn't have time to waste. Equipped with a small scythe, a crowbar, and a bundle of canvas bags, he set out towards the rice fields a mile away to work on the next part of his plan. Vasu was asked to keep an eye on Benjamin which she happily agreed to do.

On his way to the rice fields lay an area of tall grass and Heera worked his way through with a scythe. The trees here were few and far between, and the Indian sun filtered through the gaps between tree tops, warming patches of grass unevenly. These warm patches were of particular interest to Heera because he knew that snakes loved warmth. He had come snake-catching.

After looking around, Heera spotted a brown tree snake basking in the sunshine on a rock at the bottom of a tree.

Perfect. Just what I need.

Heera squatted next to the snake, just a foot away, admiring the brown stripes on its body.

"Won't hurt you, I promise," he whispered. The reptile didn't move. Heera picked the snake up by its tail with his bare hands and lowered it into his canvas bag.

"I'll set you free soon." And he set off towards the paddy fields.

Within twenty minutes of searching the rice fields, Heera spotted a medium-sized striped snake which he recognised as a non-venomous keelback snake, concealed under the bark of a fence post, its brown markings barely visible against the wood. Skilfully, he manoeuvred the snake into a canvas bag like he had done earlier.

It was dusk by the time Heera returned home, triumphant – he had managed to find three striking, non-venomous snakes, a sack full of sandy soil he had managed to gather from near a creek in the forest, three uprooted plants of turmeric, and a handful of fresh grass. Actually, he had come across over thirteen snakes that day, but most had been the venomous type. That's not what he had wanted and so he let them go.

A delicious aroma of spices leaked from the hut; Vasu was cooking his favourite potato curry and brown rice. At any other time, the smell of his mother's cooking at the end of a tiring day would have made Heera hungry enough to eat a horse. However, his mind was brimming with planning the tasks he had lined up for that evening and the anticipation and the possibilities of tomorrow. His stomach was practically on strike.

Heera quickly checked on Benjamin and threw him a handful of green grass. Then he crept towards the back of the hut, found an earthen pot and half-filled it with the sandy soil from his sack. Carefully, he let the snakes into the pot, and tied the mouth of the pot with jute so that the reptiles couldn't escape but had air to breathe.

There. All done. He dusted the sand off his hands and wiped the rest on his *dhoti*.

"Heera, is it you?" Vasu had heard him outside.

"Coming, Ma." He picked Benjamin up and carried him inside in one arm propped against his chest, with the other holding the plants and green grass.

"Here, Ma." He held out the turmeric. "I got you some haldi. I can grind it for you tonight if you like." Heera glanced at the stone slab beside Vasu. She generally put it at the back of the hut but this time it was inside.

Vasu stopped stirring the curry and looked at him in disbelief. Her lips gave way to a smile.

"That would be great, Son. Look what I've made. Your favourite potato curry. Come and eat."

Vasu served him a portion of rice and steaming curry on a banana leaf. And Heera tried to eat with the enthusiasm his mother would have expected of him.

The thought of the anklet floated back to him. *Should I ask her now?*

"Have you eaten, Ma?"

"I'll have some a bit later. Not very hungry. I had some while cooking; you know I have to taste a bit to make sure the salt is right," Vasu lied.

Heera was used to his mother fussing about how full she was, either by eating fruits she had found in the forest while collecting wood, or by eating while she cooked. They were all lies. He had it figured out ever since he was big enough to realise it wasn't the vermillion saree that had made his mother cry.

"Here," he said mixing some rice with curry, rolling it into a tiny ball onto the tips of his bare fingers and held out the morsel to his mother. "I can feed you now."

Vasu swatted at his wrist. "You eat–"

"Come on, Ma." He forced it into her mouth. "Ma… can I ask you something?" His skin prickled. Vasu nodded chewing on the food in her mouth. "Why didn't you tell me about the silver anklet?"

Vasu made a coughing sound like something had blocked her throat. She cleared it.

"Wh– what anklet?"

"The one in the trunk."

Vasu looked tensely in the direction of the trunk, then forced herself to relax into a smile.

"Oh that! It's yours."

"Mine? Then why didn't you tell me about it?" Heera asked.

"What do you mean?" Vasu stood up to pour water into an earthen cup. Heera had caught on to her unease. She avoided his eyes.

"Ma…" Heera's tone was firm. Vasu looked at him after placing down the cup of water beside the banana leaf he was eating from. He sounded grown, his voice deeper and cracking at the edges. "You know what I mean."

"It's just an anklet. Why are you making a mountain out of it? You wore it when you were younger; a baby."

"It's not *just* an anklet. It's *the* anklet I see in my dreams."

Vasu gave out a hollow chuckle, like a tuneless bell. "How would I know that?"

"You would because I told you... at least a million times. I described it–"

"Oh, come on, Heera." Vasu threw her hands out in frustration. "Are you saying I'm lying?"

Heera's head fell. He knew Mother was impenetrable at times, but he didn't want to hurt her. *It's nothing. She must have been too tired to remember the anklet I described.* It felt like a lie. Or perhaps not. His mind oscillated between the two. But soon Heera decided to focus on the present.

Before going to bed, he ground the turmeric roots into a fine paste and collected it in a small earthen jar. His fingers had been stained yellow and reeked of the gingery, peppery smell of turmeric. Benjamin had fallen asleep, in a corner of the hut, full and satisfied from the meal of fresh grass.

Heera forced his eyes shut. Next day he was going to meet Bali. It had been long enough already, and he couldn't wait.

Chapter Fifteen

A little brown baby boy was bawling at the top of his lungs, standing naked on a ledge in the forest that was draped with curtains of mist. The only thing the baby had on its body was a silver anklet. Heera knew that the baby was in pain, extreme agony. But he didn't know what had caused it. He ached to hold it. But no matter how hard he tried he couldn't get himself to climb the ledge and reach the baby. Sweat trickled from his forehead. He tried but his legs wouldn't move as fast as he wished them to and, when he reached the ledge, it was too slippery to hold on to. Frustration screamed in his chest, and he tried with all his might, but he fell back down every single time. He used his hands and feet and nails and even teeth, losing a few, but nothing worked.

Heera felt a cool wet touch at his ear. It was

Bali's trunk, he knew, until it started nibbling at his earlobe with small sharp teeth. Heera wondered why he hadn't seen those teeth inside Bali's trunk. How come that knowledge had eluded him for so long? Peeved with his lack of observation, he pushed Bali's trunk away. However, it wasn't what it used to be. The trunk had grown a dense coat of fine, soft hair on it, fluffy to the touch. *What?*

Heera touched his ear and jerked back into reality. Benjamin had been nibbling at it. Sweaty and sullen, he sat up, scowling at Benjamin. *It's you.* Fanning himself with the end of the straw mat he had been lying on, he wiped the sweat off his forehead and face with the back of his upper arm. He swallowed and his dry and parched throat cracked and hurt.

He put Benjamin on his lap and stroked his fleecy coat. Nerves rippled through every inch of his body at the thought of Bali.

It had been eight sunrises since Bali had been captured, the sunrise of that day being the ninth and yet to happen. Heera inhaled deeply. This was the day he had been looking forward to. There was nothing more he wanted than to see Bali. And yet he feared he wouldn't like what he found. The concoction of apprehension, anxiety and excitement formed a solid lump in the pit of his stomach. No matter how much he tried stroking it away, it didn't help.

It was long before dawn. Vasu was asleep.

Heera tiptoed out of the hut with the jar full of turmeric paste, making sure Benjamin was still inside. Sitting outside, he wrapped his head with the vermillion saree cloth and put the kajal around his eyes. Fetching his canvas bag from behind the hut, he gently tipped the snakes from the pot into the sack. Next, he bundled the leaves of the turmeric plant and set off on a run to the location where Bali was being held.

It was a five-kilometre jog and the muscles in his thighs burned with exhaustion. He had made it before first light.

He climbed a tree to gain a vantage point. It was still quite dark although the deep blue sky had started to lighten, streaking the horizon orange and purple. The moon was already saying goodbye.

The two makeshift shelters occupied by the village men stood a couple of metres away from the enclosure that held Bali. There were no men to be seen around, much to Heera's relief. Between the enclosure and the make-do shelters was a gulmohar tree, its flaming red flowers dulled in the weak light of the early morning hours. Two huge patches of buzzing blackness dangled at different heights from the tree top. *Beehives!*

The air was thick with the sweet aroma of honey. Heera's mouth watered. He was accustomed to climbing to hives and helping himself to a piece of honeycomb without disturbing the bees too much. Prior to climbing, he would coat his body with the sap of the tonyoge plant and the bees would remain docile around him. But today wasn't the time for that.

The enclosure was covered by a huge asbestos sheet and open on all sides, framed by wooden logs that made a kind of fence. Inside, Bali lay on a carpet of straw.

Heera's heart leaped with joy and twisted with sorrow at the same time. All he wanted to do was go and embrace Bali. This was his chance. Before anybody could see him.

He entered the pen, checking all directions. There was nobody. Only deep stillness.

Bali lay asleep, his chest rising and falling. He shifted a bit, picking up Heera's scent.

Kneeling at Bali's head, Heera caressed the rough hide on Bali's face and ears in long gentle strokes with his quivering hands. The golden-brown eyes opened halfway, foggy from exhaustion and pain. It was unusual for Bali to be asleep at this hour. Heera instantly recognised it wasn't sleep that kept Bali from standing up. His despair tightened around his chest in a vice-like grip.

Bali tried raising his head, but it was too much of an effort and it went down like a log, shaking the ground under Heera. Tears rampantly spilled from Heera's eyes, dripping onto Bali's skin. His heart bled. Calluses had formed on Bali's rear leg that had been chained. There was a tear on his ear that had formed a scab. The magnificent elephant that roamed the forest uninhibited had been reduced to a pitiable lump of misery; a prisoner.

"I'm sorry, I couldn't protect you. Forgive me, Bali," he whispered.

Heera ached to cradle Bali like a baby in his arms. How he wished he could sever the chains and walk Bali to his freedom. But, as he had suspected, this was the wrong time. Even if he could cut the chains, Bali wouldn't be able to run away from his captors. And that was precisely why Heera had come to him. To nurse him, to make him stronger and to free him eventually. And now that he had his ticket to freedom – Benjamin – he felt confident and hopeful about doing what he had planned.

Heera buried his face into Bali's ear. Through the bone, deep and warm, vibrated a throaty rumble. It was the kind of sound nobody could hear, only feel. And Heera knew for certain that Bali was glad. Happy in his presence.

Heera stroked Bali's head and then outstretched himself and lay parallel to his belly. He knew he didn't have much time but, even if it was for a moment, it was worth it.

I'm really sorry for what I'm about to do now, Bali. But I promise it's to set things right.

Heera walked away and opened the sack full of snakes where Bali couldn't see him and let them out around Bali. Guilt surged through him, as he watched himself do what he'd have never even dreamed of doing otherwise, knowing that elephants hated snakes. And Heera knew Bali hardly even had the strength to move.

The snakes slithered around Bali who immediately sensed them and flinched. Heera stood back. He could feel a cold wave of panic rising in Bali and a knot twisted his insides knowing that he was the cause of it. However, there was no other way he could think of. All he needed was a trumpet big enough to wake the men in the shelters.

Come on. Give me a huge bellow.

A snake wriggled on Bali's rear foot and Bali shook his leg violently and cried. Heera's face tingled with guilt. He wrestled to hold himself back from lunging forward and moving the snake, to relieve Bali. However, they were harmless, he knew, and that's why he had chosen the non-venomous ones.

One more, Bali, come on. He ran outside to see if any men had woken.

By now Bali was panicking, desperately trying to

rise up but unable to. The agonising sight was cutting through Heera's heart like an ice-cold sickle. He only hoped what he intended would work. *Come on.* And then Bali let out a wild trumpet that would have woken a village. The chain around his rear leg went taut and then slackened, clanking against the metal pole he had been tied to. He squirmed around in a frenzy.

I'm so, so sorry.

Noises started to fill the silence; doors opening, footfalls and agitated voices. The men were awake.

"That's it. That's it. We're done now. Easy. Easy." Heera spoke at the top of his voice on purpose, pretending to be oblivious to the men.

The crunching sound of footfalls over leaves neared. He quickly put the bundle of turmeric leaves inside the sack he had used to carry the snakes and left it on the floor. Then he darted towards a snake and grabbed it.

"Got you. How dare you trouble an innocent animal." He looked at Bali. "Calm down! It won't harm you now. I've got it."

Bali let out a leaden groan, relaxing his rear foot, and the chain slackened down with a clank. Heera's eyes flew to Bali's rear foot and another, harder knot formed in his stomach. Bali had yanked his leg with the metal chain around it, hysterical from seeing the snake, causing the already sore calluses on his foot to bleed. Heera's face flushed with the realisation. How would he ever forgive himself?

"Hey! Who're you?" The words of a bare-chested man in a dhoti gashed through his blanket of shame, making him jump.

"There are snakes here." Heera pushed away the tightening feeling in his stomach and held out his hand with the snake in it, brandishing it. "That's why Ba– I mean, the elephant is shrieking. It's making him nervous."

"How did you get here?" another man asked.

"Shh! Hang on. There are more," Heera warned. "Get me a pot or a sack. Quick." His tone was pressing and urgent. The two men fumbled around anxiously. Bali was whimpering.

"What happened? What's going on?" A third man came in floundering. He was older than the first two men with a thick white moustache that almost hid his lips.

"Snakes! There are snakes here."

"Here! Take this." One of them threw Heera a jute sack and Heera put the snake inside it.

"Here…" Heera said, holding out the sack to the man who took it with shaky hands. "Just hold it shut!"

Heera ran towards the other snake before it got closer to Bali. What he wanted had been accomplished and he had caused enough damage to his friend. He couldn't look Bali in the eye and kept his gaze low.

Another man burst into the pen with a solid, tall bamboo stick. The increasing light of dawn turned him into a dark silhouette. There were now four men in total in the pen with Heera and Bali.

"Where are the snakes? Let's kill them!" The man said, thumping his stick hard on the ground in a fit of rage.

Heera cringed. That was the last thing he wanted. The snakes had helped him. He couldn't let these men kill them. Absolutely not.

"Step back. They're dangerous," he cautioned.

The other three men faltered backwards.

The third snake Heera had released had slithered off. He was secretly glad he had been sensible enough to get a few of them.

"Let's burn them." The man with the stick shouted, galvanising the other two young men into action. His body was toned and muscular.

Heera could taste the fear in the back of his throat. On the day Bali was captured, this man was one of the shikaris who'd pinned his arms behind his back and shaken him violently by the tuft of his hair. Goose bumps sprung up on his body.

"Yes, Mangal. Come on," one of the two young men asserted.

"NO!" Heera couldn't help blurting out, almost

mechanically.

Mangal flashed a hard stare at him. "Who're *you*?"

Heera dropped his head to look at the snake in his hands. Although he had been covered in a slush of thick gooey mud that day when Bali had been captured, he hoped Mangal did not look close enough.

As if on cue, Mangal came closer to Heera and a tinge of recognition flashed in his eyes, but then he looked away, distracted by the man with the thick white moustache.

"Give him a sack, someone." The old man signalled to the two young men.

Heera drew a deep breath and shook himself out of the worry shrouding his mind like a thick fog.

"I'll take care of them. Some tribal people I know need snake venom to make medicines. I catch snakes for them. Leave all that to me. But how did they get here? The elephant could have died with one bite of this lethal snake." Heera deliberately held the snake just behind its mouth. It revealed its fangs. The men gaped.

He put the snake in the sack given to him, thanking the reptile mentally as he guided the second one in. He knotted the mouth of the sack and put it next to the other sack with the turmeric leaves in it.

The men looked at each other. Heera could sense mild panic on their faces. However, Mangal looked surly.

"Who're you?" Mangal asked. The question relaxed Heera. It meant he hadn't been recognised for sure. "How did you get here?"

"Oh– I'm Heera. I was passing by–"

"At this unearthly hour?"

"Not really unearthly. It's dawn – the best time to look for herbs. Nice and fresh. My mother makes herbal medicines." Heera took the bundle of turmeric leaves out of the sack. "Look. *Haldi.*" His tone was innocent.

The men nodded. Mangal didn't. But Heera was encouraged to continue.

"I recognise every whimper and cry elephants make. It's a language of its own. My father was a mahout and I was raised with elephants around me, you see." Heera tried not to get too carried away with his story. "This is a fine elephant. Whose is it?"

"That's not your business," Mangal scorned.

"And where is his *mahout*?" Heera took no heed of Mangal's arrogance.

"He doesn't have one... yet," answered the oldest of them, called Hariya. He was the main person in charge of Bali.

"No *mahout*! My father used to say that an elephant without a *mahout* is like a body with no soul. Dead."

"So, you're saying that the elephants in the wild

are dead… *without* mahouts." Mangal sniggered and the two young men followed.

"Mangal." Hariya glowered at him.

"Actually, I asked Father the same question." Heera smiled innocently. "He said that in the wild they're with mother nature. The interaction with her is flawless." Heera kept his tone neutral. He knew Mangal was trying to pick on him. "Only the elephants with humans need to be read, you know, just like you read books. And *only* a mahout can do that."

"Your father seems knowledgeable." Hariya smiled wisely.

Heera nodded and added, "The owner would have been terribly upset if… something untoward had happened to such a fine creature." Heera paused to watch their colourless faces as the other two men shivered at the thought of Major Crook finding out about the incident. "Thank goodness all is well now. But he does need a mahout as soon as possible." Mangal looked miffed but Hariya was not too perturbed.

Mangal gave a snort of laughter. "We don't need a child to tell us what needs doing."

"Hush, Mangal," Hariya said, trying to placate him.

"Erm… Just saying." A faintly nervous chuckle escaped Heera's mouth. "A well looked after and

135

trained elephant is his owner's delight. I'm just telling you what I know. You never know… your boss may well be pleased enough to reward you all." Heera crossed his fingers and hoped that he had made a point.

Mangal was gawking as if he had never thought about what had just been said. He had a fine chance at impressing the Major.

"Hmm… where's your father?" Hariya enquired. "Maybe he could help us then." He looked at Bali and then back at Heera who had turned to Bali, itching to address the wound on his rear leg.

"Father died," Heera heard himself say. That was the only single piece of truth he had uttered that morning. His memories of his father were faint.

"Oh… I'm sorry," Hariya said.

"Look, he's bleeding. I can dress his wound, if you like." Heera hurried, without waiting for an affirmative answer, to get his earthen jar full of turmeric paste. He crouched beside Bali's rear leg that had been bleeding from the sore calluses. *I'm so sorry. I'll fix it. Forgive me.*

"Wait. I'll do it," Mangal said sternly. "Being a mahout is no big deal. I can take care of the elephant." The idea to please the Major was baking hot in his head.

Heera didn't want to, but he stepped back and watched Mangal grab Bali's rear foot.

Bali rumbled raucously, lifting his head with great effort. His tusks pointed at Mangal intimidatingly. Mangal jerked away, humiliated.

"Insolent wild beast. Get me my bamboo stick," Mangal shouted. "He needs a good beating – to be taught a lesson."

"NO! No… Gentle. You need to be gentle," Heera insisted, fighting to keep his tone placid when his blood was boiling.

"You don't tell me what to do," Mangal snapped.

"I- I don't mean to–"

"Mangal." Hariya spoke with a composure that didn't compromise the firmness he intended. Mangal stepped back tetchily. "We wouldn't want sahib to see this…"

"Can I try once? You can then do as you please, if it doesn't work."

Hariya nodded.

Heera had heaved a sigh of relief for being allowed to dress Bali's wounds when the mention of *sahib* made his skin tingle with anger. He bent down and stroked Bali's leg. Bali let out a mellow rumble, acknowledging Heera. The men were taken aback at the contrasting reaction the animal had had to Mangal just moments ago. Heera began to apply turmeric paste over Bali's wound and wrapped it with turmeric leaves.

The men, along with Hariya, walked a little

further away from him but Heera could still overhear bits of their conversation as they murmured amongst themselves, behind him.

"–We need one – the boy's a natural–"

"–he's only a child –"

"–who cares – he seems to know what he's doing–"

"–come on Mangal. *Sahib* will be pleased – he wants the elephant healthy and tamed–"

Then Hariya ambled back towards Heera and stood beside him.

"I'm sure you'll make a fine mahout one day… just like your father." Hariya's lips widened under his thick white moustache in what may have been a smile. "And you're not wrong in saying the elephant needs a mahout. So perhaps you could be one to him?"

Heera's heart leaped. It looked like he had hit the spot.

Hariya continued. "I can see you have a natural flair for it. Will you be willing to help us take care of this elephant?"

Heera's heart vaulted in his chest. *YES*, he wanted to scream. But he sealed his lips shut.

"Me?!" Heera faked his surprise.

"Hmm…" Hariya nodded.

"Erm– I–" Heera wondered what words to use, to not look too keen. And at the same time, to not decline the offer either. His heart was drumming with joy. But he had to work hard to conceal it and not jump at the opportunity.

"You'll do well… I'm sure."

"Well, my foot!" Mangal hissed and spat at the ground before walking out of the pen.

"Don't worry about him," Hariya reassured. "He's a hot-head, you'll make a fine mahout. But there's… a problem." Heera cringed. "I cannot hire you…" Heera's heart gave a jolt. *After all this?* "What I mean is…" Hariya continued. Heera was all ears. "Only *sahib* can. And he'll hire you only when he sees how good you are. Which I'm sure you are. But you'll need to prove yourself before you get paid. Do you understand me?"

Hariya had exactly worded what Heera was aiming for. All this while he had wanted to be with Bali as his *mahout* and he had been trying to find a way to do it. And what better way than letting the Major see him prove his prowess. This was much better than him approaching the Major on his own, even with recommendations. The money was the least of his concerns and the last thing on his mind. He wanted Bali to heal before he could free him. And he already had his insurance, Benjamin, in case things went wrong.

Heera didn't want to push his luck any more. And before Hariya could open his mouth to say more, he nodded and let the words tumble out. "I'll give it a shot. But I'll need to be home when it's dark as mother won't let me stay here overnight. I can come early morning though and stay till dusk."

Hariya nodded. "That's fine."

"I love elephants… like my father did. Only this time I'll do it all by myself. But I'll do my best not to disappoint you." He flashed his innocent eyes at Hariya.

Hariya smiled. "You may start tomorrow."

At the thought of being with Bali, a huge wave of happiness swayed and swelled inside Heera until he thought he might burst. He turned away from the man and looked at Bali. And burst into a smile big enough to make his cheeks hurt.

Heera would have loved to start the very same day. But tomorrow was better than never, he decided, although a thought pricked him: Bali needed to eat else he would languish. Even a day could make a difference.

He turned back to face the old man and cleared his throat. "Of course. I'll be here at first light tomorrow. But before I leave, can I feed the elephant some of these turmeric leaves? They'll help prevent any infection in the wound and he needs strength to recover."

"Yes. Why not?" Hariya smiled. "I'll leave you to it."

Heera joined his palms in a namaste. "Thank you, for the job." Hariya turned his back and ambled away with the two men beside him.

Heera beamed at Bali and threw his arms around his head, once the men were out of sight. The warm hold of wrinkly skin engulfed him: Bali's trunk.

The only thing left to sort out was... Mother. Heera ran home, head over heels.

Chapter Sixteen

Heera had lied to Vasu about getting a job gathering cinnamon and turmeric for a spice merchant. That gave him enough reason to stay out all day in the forest peeling bark – which was laborious but Bali's favourite food – and collecting grass, leaves, and turmeric plant roots for Bali's wounds, and the rest of the day feeding Bali and dressing his wounds. Although he felt sorry about lying, it was easier than convincing Mother. Moreover, Vasu was glad to see Heera moving on with his life, instead of brooding over Bali. It certainly was more of a presumption she made rather than the reality.

To watch Bali recover was heartening. Apart from the wound on his leg, Bali had many cuts and scabs on his back and ears, from being poked with iron rods. Every new wound that Heera discovered jabbed his heart and set off a thunderstorm of fury in his head.

His passion amazed Hariya and the other men around, but it annoyed Mangal more and more. Bali was up on his fours by the end of the third day. And he looked stronger and well by the end of the week.

"I've named him Bali," Heera told Hariya who had come to check on them. "It's after Bajrang Bali."

Hariya nodded. "It's good. Well-fitting." He smiled showing no lips; more with his white moustache.

"Watch this," Heera said. He stroked Bali's head between his eyes and gripped both tusks firmly. "UP! UP!" Bali cocked his head back, lifting Heera off the ground, and moved his head from side to side with Heera dangling off his tusks.

"Wow! That's amazing. He has a sure liking for you, son."

"Oh. So, when did we have a naming ceremony then… for *BALI?*" Mangal mocked. A smirk stirred on his face as he swaggered in behind Hariya.

"Mangal, why don't you get Bali some water from the well," Hariya said.

"Ask the mahout. Isn't *he* supposed to be doing it?"

"He's just a child, Mangal. It takes strength to pull buckets full of water from the well. And the well is quite far away, don't you know? We've run out. Now go." Mangal scoffed and kicked the fence of the pen, leaving stormily.

A week later, an Indian servant called Mani came bursting in through the living room door and screeched to a halt in front of Major Cook.

"Sahib, good news, sahib."

Mani was the main caretaker of the bungalow and nothing like the butlers the Queen or the Lords in Britain have. On the contrary, he was not even half as polished, raw as a stone slab and as talkative as a magpie. However, he tried to restrain his tongue in the Major's presence.

The Major was slumped on a velvet couch, with one leg on an ornately carved sandalwood table, brooding over his loss of Benjamin with a peg of whisky at midday. He had forgotten about the elephant he had caught.

Crook looked up, blood-shot eyes rolling, unmoored by the intoxication. "Did ya find him?" he slurred. "Benji…"

"No serr–" The man's 'r's rolled sharply as the words spilled out in an Indian accent.

"Then what is good 'bout it you bloody fool!" The Major flopped back dejected, his head and hands hanging loose like a rag doll.

"Sahib, mahout found sahib. For elephant."

"WHO?"

"A *mahout*, sahib."

144

"Whooz da mahout I meant, *you fool.*"

"The boy, sahib. He good, *sahib.*" Mani's 'd's were as hard-hitting and jarring as his 'r's. "He has animal wrapped around his foot, sahib." Mani was over-enthusiastic with English phrases but he rarely, if ever, got them right.

"*Finger* not foot!" Crook was drunk but not drunk enough not to catch a mistake with his mother tongue. "Blithering idiot," he murmured, standing up and stumbling forward.

"Sahib… careful." Mani stepped forward to support Crook.

"Keep yer hands off me." Crook waved his limp arms in protest. Mani hesitated and stepped back. "Take me there," Crook demanded, and dropped onto his couch and fell asleep.

Late afternoon the next day, in the distance, the sound of galloping horse hooves caught Heera's attention. There was a surge of disquiet around him amongst the men.

"*Sahib* is coming," one of them shouted. It seemed Crook had been too distracted the past week looking for and missing his pet rabbit, just as Heera had hoped. But now fear and anxiety undulated through Heera.

The horse's gallop died down to a trot. Its harness jingled and its saddle creaked as the horse's gait slowed.

"*Sahib*, welcome." Mangal said in a heavy Indian accent, kowtowing to Crook. "Please come."

Heera could tell it was Mangal and by the tone of his voice he could tell the intention was flattery.

The Major dismounted, leather squeaking as he grabbed the pommel.

"This way, sahib," Mangal said, whirling around the Major like an excited bumble bee around a flower.

"Out of my way," Crook growled and Mangal fell back mortified.

Heera touched his eyes as if he could have felt the kajal and adjusted his turban, bracing himself to face the Major.

The sound of steel-capped boots on gravel reverberated through the pen. Heera fussed around with the grass and the pile of straw around Bali, trying to look busy. The drumming of the boots got louder until they stopped and he realised he was sharing the space with his enemy. Goose bumps covered his body. Time slowed to a stop.

"The animal is behaving now, aye," Crook said, raising his chin high in Bali's direction – he was munching on some grass.

Mangal nodded, although with less enthusiasm than before.

Heera looked at the Major from the corner of his

eye. The lines on his forehead looked deeper and his face more worn than he had noticed the first time. A grey-black stubble now covered the lower part of his face, making him look older, as if he had aged ten years in just over a week.

"*Janwar*," Crook said, spilling disdain. "He's learned his lesson." Coming from Crook, the word *janwar* sounded outlandish to Heera but even more offensive.

Bali. Heera throbbed with ire. *His name is Bali*.

"Stubborn beast... had to be set right," Crook added.

Crook had been speaking as if Heera didn't exist. That's not what Heera had expected; although it was better than being recognised. And as he thought this, the Major spoke again. This time looking straight at Heera.

"You over there... Who're you?" The Major clicked his fingers arrogantly.

Heera was forced to look up at him. His brain went blank for a moment.

"The *mahout*?" Crook peered at Heera in surprise, stroking his stubble.

Heera only understood the last word and guessed what the Major had asked. He nodded vacuously. It helped to look stupid when expecting trouble, he decided. Inside, his nerves raged like a tempestuous ocean.

"Yes, Sahib." Hariya lumbered behind dragging his aged body as fast as he could, just in time. "He talk no English, sahib." He stopped to catch his breath and pointed to Heera.

"He's just a boy!" Crook turned to Hariya. "So, you're telling me a *boy* did what four grown men couldn't?" He scoffed.

Mangal discreetly shot Heera a look of revulsion. The other men stood still in the background like superfluous creatures.

"Er – he grew with elephant, sahib. He–" Hariya explained in his calm manner, but stopped mid-sentence.

Crook had dismissed him with an impatient wave of his hand. The corner of his mouth lifted into a lopsided smirk. "As long as the beast is healthy and behaving. Who'd pay for a lofty, bad-tempered elephant?" Crook pivoted on his heels and strutted out with Hariya trailing behind him.

Heera heaved a sigh, relieved at the Major's departure.

"Aye – whatever – just throw something at the lad," Heera heard the Major say apathetically.

"Shukriya, sahib," Hariya replied.

Soon, there was a clank of the saddle and the departing gallop of horse hooves. Heera wiped his sweaty palms on his dhoti.

"You've earned yourself a job, son." Hariya

returned, beaming. "Although don't know how long it'll last..." Hariya looked at Bali. "Looks like this fine creature will be sold soon."

Heera faltered. That last sentence had cut the ground from under his feet.

Chapter Seventeen

Heera sat with Benjamin on his lap, stroking his silky fur, wondering if it was time to negotiate a deal with the Major; trade Bali in exchange for Benjamin. But how and when? He held out a portion of grass and Benjamin keenly nibbled on it.

Vasu looked at the two in admiration and left for the forest that stood still below a violet sky blushing into pinks and peaches.

Heera hadn't slept well. Not that he had since Bali was taken away, but the previous night had been a fog of confusion and worry. His mind was twirling with thoughts of Bali being sold. Flashes of dreams with the crying child wearing the silver anklet bothered him.

Digging at Hariya for details about when and to whom Bali was being sold had been fruitless. Nobody was sure what the Major had in mind.

Heera set off to the forest, wanting to gather some wild sugarcane for Bali.

Being a tribal boy, he couldn't enter the Hanuman temple on his way to the forest, so he blinked a prayer from a distance. *Bajrang Bali, please help me free Bali. I don't want him to be sold and live in slavery.*

A familiar face near the temple smiled at him. It was Maya. She was holding a thali of fresh flowers, kumkum, and incense sticks in one hand and waving with the other.

Heera waved back.

Maya had started to walk towards him before he could leave so he stayed put.

When she was close enough, Heera harrumphed, unable to decide what to say. "Going to offer your prayers, then?"

Maya nodded and smiled teasingly. "Do you want me to ask God for something for you?" Her black hair doused with coconut oil glistened in the early morning sun. She smelled of the jasmines in her thali.

Heera half-smiled, shaking his head, and looked at the temple, going through a range of retorts in his head and wondering which one to choose. Then he said something entirely different. "I remembered… last year… in the forest – you with the cobra."

"Finally! I'm honoured." Maya chuckled. Heera

remained silent. Then she confessed, "Took me a moment too, to recognise you that day. I think it was your hair. It's a bit–" she tried to find the right word to use for his irregularly cut hair, finally settling on, "– different. It was longer, then." She hurriedly said the last sentence as if hoping to camouflage the word 'different' in it.

"Umm... yes," Heera ran his fingers through his short hair. He remembered the vow he had taken.

"Long hair suits you," she blurted out, blushing immediately. "Erm... Not that this looks bad. Either is good."

Awkward at being scrutinised, Heera's eyes flitted from Maya to the temple to the tree near the temple and back to Maya, never settling on anything for longer than a fraction of a second.

"So... found your elephant then?" Maya said it more like telling than asking.

Heera nodded. "Thank you for helping that day. Raju told you?"

Maya's face fell at the mention of Raju's name. "Hmm."

"What's wrong?"

Maya looked away from him. "Raju... He doesn't have a home to live in anymore."

"What do you mean? Doesn't he live behind the Major's bungalow? In the servants' quarters?"

Maya shook her head. "He and his Baba were

thrown out."

"What? Why?"

"The Major accused Baba of stealing Benjamin."

"What?" Heera felt like a boulder had been placed on his chest. He knew that wasn't the truth.

"The Major has lost his mind, ever since Benjamin has gone missing." Maya's face flushed crimson and she spat out the words like bitter seeds. "They found Baba's lighter there – in the room where Benjamin was kept in his cage."

"Lighter? What's that?" Heera didn't know that the tool he had used to set fire to the Major's car was called a lighter.

Maya explained and the events of that night came swirling back into Heera's mind. He had used a lighter to set the car on fire and probably left it in the Major's dressing room where Benjamin had been kept.

"How was the Major so sure that it was Baba's lighter?" he enquired.

What Heera was sure of was that he had acquired the lighter after it had fallen from a servant's pocket; a young man, whom he had seen while hiding in the shrubs at the periphery of the bungalow. That man couldn't have been Baba as, from what Raju had said, Baba was aged. Heera wasn't sure if he had left the lighter in the dressing room. And if he had, was it really Baba's? Perhaps the young servant – whom he remembered was called Ramlal – had borrowed Baba's lighter. His mind was a tangled mess of thoughts.

"He was the only one amongst the staff at the bungalow to own a lighter, gifted to him by another English officer he had served earlier on in his days as a sepoy." Maya gulped and quelled a sniffle at the same time.

Heera felt sick, his stomach folding onto itself. He had inadvertently put Raju and his Baba in trouble. Whoever's lighter it was, all that mattered was that the brunt of the whole act was taken by Baba who was wrongly accused and punished, and so was Raju, when the person to blame was him.

And as if that wasn't enough, Maya spoke again. "His Baba was whipped and kicked..." Her voice cracked amongst sobs. "He's in a poor state..." She trailed off.

This was unbearable; the guilt churning within Heera had grown into a mountain, crushing him under it. How would he ever look Raju in the eye?

Baba is everything to me. Raju's words came back to him like pelting stones.

Had he almost orphaned an orphan again? His chest tightened making it difficult for him to breathe. How could he have been so reckless?

"So where is Raju now?" Heera asked, forcing himself to speak.

"They're both at my house." Maya sniffed and wiped her nose with the end of her flowing skirt. She cleared her throat and added, "But I don't see how this can continue much longer... They need a home."

"Is Raju–" Heera couldn't find the right word. 'Okay' or 'all right' didn't fit. How could Raju be okay after all this?

"He won't leave his Baba's side. No more street shows... he did them with his macaque to earn some paisa and aid his Baba since Baba hardly ever made money at the bungalow. But, at the moment, Raju is too shaken to do anything. He won't leave Baba's side."

Heera empathised with Raju's pain.

A lump swelled inside his throat. He was the cause of a catastrophe in someone's life.

Maya put her hands together, entwined her fingers and spoke passionately, as if the intensity of her speech would manifest what she was saying. "How I wish Benjamin is found soon. At least then the Major will hopefully restore Baba's and Raju's lives back and they can then have a roof over their heads and food on their plates."

A staunch 'yes' arose within Heera. It was time to come clean.

"Take me to your house... this evening," Heera said with clarity this time, although his tone was laden with remorse. "Please. I would like to see Raju and his Baba."

Maya nodded. "Meet me here at sunset."

Chapter Eighteen

After offering Bali the sugarcane he had gathered that morning from the forest, Heera's mind strayed to Raju.

"What should I do, Bali?" he asked, stroking Bali's face below his eyes. Bali bobbed his head as if to an inaudible beat, eagerly chewing on sugarcane, relishing every mouthful of sweetness. "I know... I've messed up everything and I have to fix it. I want to. But how?"

Heera was too distracted to notice Mangal come into the pen.

"Ah, sugarcane!" Heera was startled out of his trail of thoughts by Mangal's sneer. "Whose fields have you robbed?"

"Why would I steal? I'm no thief." Heera replied with a glower. He turned away to fetch some more sugarcane for Bali. "The forest is open to everyone.

One should know where to look."

"You sure know where to look then, don't you?" Mangal tapped the side of his nose with his index finger to accompany his derisive stare. Heera got the creeps. It felt as if he meant much more than the words he had uttered. Mangal paced away, leaving Heera in a pool of doubt.

Soon Heera's thoughts again drifted back to Raju and Baba. The feeling of doubt didn't seem as significant as the guilt whipping inside him.

That evening, Maya played with the ends of her braids while pacing the length of the wall at the back of the Hanuman temple.

"You're late," she said, irritated on seeing Heera.

"I'm sorry. Was held up." Heera had taken a longer route to the temple on purpose. Since the day before, he had the funny feeling of being watched. And he didn't know if it was a fact or his own mind playing games on him. He thought a longer route would shake off a stalker; if there was one at all.

The two walked towards Maya's house.

Heera walked as if he was alone, in silence.

Maya, on the other hand, was overflowing with questions, wondering how to start and what to ask first. "Raju told me about you following him," Maya said, finally failing to quell her urge to speak. "To the Major's bungalow." Heera remained silent. "You're not afraid of anything are you? Not of snakes, not even the Major!"

"I didn't know it was the Major's bungalow then," Heera replied. "I was only following Raju like you told me to."

"I asked you to follow him to Bali, not the lion's den." Maya glared. Heera didn't reply. "Anyways, and now you're Bali's new mahout, aren't you? Raju said he had heard it. He guessed it must have been you, since–"

"Since I had told him about my intentions of being a mahout," Heera completed abruptly. "Yes, that's me."

Maya looked at him with wonder-struck eyes. "You *are* brave. Didn't you think of what could happen if the Major finds out?"

How Heera wished she could be quiet. He wanted to be left on his own. There was nothing more for him to say until he saw Raju and his Baba. He felt far from *brave*, then.

"How far is it?" he asked.

"Oh! My house? We're almost there."

The sun had started to set and dip at the horizon. By the time they arrived at Maya's house, the sky was a hue of navy blue.

"That's my house," Maya pointed at the dim light of a diya, flickering through a window in a wall plastered with earth.

Maya knocked on a small wooden door – the kind with two shutters that opened in the middle. The door looked like it had been painted a shade of sky blue at least a century ago. Warped by the sun and rain, it also had lesions of time and over-use on it.

The pungent, spicy smell of mustard and curry leaf seasoning along, with a muffled hacking, filtered through the worn wood of the door and it creaked open unleashing the smells and sounds behind it, heightening them in an instant.

Between the shutters appeared the worn, creased face of a man with a fringe of grey hair starting at his temple and running all along the back of his head to meet his other temple, leaving a big shiny patch of scalp on the top: Maya's father.

"Where have you been?" the old man snapped; his grey brows knitted.

"Sorry Appa, I went to get–" Maya stepped aside to reveal Heera behind her.

"Who's this?" The old man grimaced.

"Appa, this is Heera." The old man blinked blankly. "The boy I told you about," Maya said emphasising her words by widening her eyes, but her father didn't yield. "The snake-boy – in the jungle last year." Heera shifted uneasily, looking like he was uncomfortable in his own skin.

"Why is he here?"

Maya threw her father a wide-eyed glare as if telling him that he sounded rude. "He's here to see Raju and his Baba."

"Come in, child," the old man spoke hurriedly in a kinder voice as if atoning for his delinquency. He threw a glance behind him. "Someone's here to see your Baba, Raju." The coughing stopped for a brief second and then continued. "He isn't too well – Raju's Baba." The old man stepped aside. "Was it Heera – your name? Come in, come in."

The corner of Heera's mouth lifted slightly into an obligatory smile, and he quickly stepped in after Maya.

Rajveer lay in a corner, on a charpai, covered in a worn, black blanket stripped red and blue. He strained to lift the upper half of his body, panting hard to catch his breath. Stroking his back, Raju tried to soothe him.

Basanti the macaque was tied to a leg of the charpai. She sat up alert, possessively chewing on the piece of bread she held.

Raju looked at Heera and his brown eyes glimmered with recognition.

Heera floundered for words.

"What are you doing here?" Raju asked before Heera could speak.

"Um… I came to see you… Maya told me… what happened." Heera's heart thudded.

Rajveer looked up at Heera with blood-shot eyes, one swollen with a nasty purple bruise around it. He strained to speak.

"Baba, you should rest. Don't talk," Raju hushed him and tucked the blanket under him, then looked at Heera with watery eyes. "He was badly beaten... for no fault of his." Rajveer grabbed Raju's wrist and shook his head.

Heera couldn't speak. It was as if his throat was packed with sand; the guilt defeating.

"Let it go... child..."

"Shh!" Raju hushed him up and wiped the spittle that had escaped his mouth while coughing off his white beard with a small piece of cotton cloth. "Rest now. No talking."

"He's... he's... like my... my mother," Rajveer gave out a titter until it needled his abdomen and his head fell back into the bed exhausted.

"Baba, easy. I told you... you need rest."

"Have some rice and dhaal with us," Maya's father said, holding a small pot of steaming rice in front of his chest. It clearly wasn't enough for all of them.

Heera had lost his appetite anyway and he shook his head.

The weight on his chest was overwhelming, his throat dry and tongue thick and fuzzy.

He knelt beside Rajveer's head on the charpai.

162

"I-I didn't know… that this would happen." He gulped not knowing what reaction was going to hit him after he had spoken the truth. "I am responsible for all of this. And I am sorry." He bowed his head. "Please forgive me."

"What is he saying?" Maya's father asked.

"What are you talking about?" Raju asked.

Finding it hard to meet his eyes, Heera looked at the floor. "I took Benjamin."

The words hung in the air, searing with truth in the tranquillity of the room fenced with gasps.

Basanti sat chin up, covertly monitoring the events around her.

It took effort but Heera lifted his gaze to meet the other boy's.

Raju's lips were pursed, his brown eyes on fire. "*You* did this? You *stole* Benjamin?"

"I'm–" Heera looked down in a long, exhausted blink and nodded. "Please forgive me." His ears, his cheeks, everything was on fire, although not showing on his brown skin.

"What were you even thinking when you came here – you'd say 'sorry' and everything would go back to as it was before? – whoosh – like a genie's magic spell?" Raju lurched at Heera and jabbed his fist into his shoulder.

Heera fell backwards from his knees onto his backside, giddy – not from the blow but from the

163

sight of something on the inside of Raju's upper arm; a tattoo. Raju had always worn shirts before, never a ganji revealing his arms. He wasn't sure, but Heera thought the tattoo looked just like his. Could Raju have belonged to a tribe like himself?

Rajveer snapped. "Raju – Calm down…" He burst into a cough.

Raju dropped his burning face into his palms. "I should have never spoken to you… never told you about Benjamin."

"Please, please… don't make it harder for me than it already is," Heera pleaded. "I'm truly sorry – I really am. And I will set it right. I promise."

"No, you *cannot*. You can't return the dignity my Baba lost – the way he was kicked and beaten, like a stray dog. Never. He's everything I've got." Raju's tone altered to a morose one. "If I lose him, I will *never* be able to forgive you. *Never*. You know what… you deserve to lose your elephant. I'm happy the Major took Bali." Raju was rampant with rage, gushing out like hot lava.

Heera stood up, steadfast, taking the bombardment with all his strength, drinking every drop of resentment.

"Raju, enough!" Rajveer chided.

"But why?" Maya asked, shocked and wide-eyed.

Heera flicked a look at Maya. "I did it for Bali."

"You put us in trouble for that stupid elephant?"

Raju cried. "May he die a rotten death. And–"

"Not… another… word," Rajveer retorted, cutting Raju off. He struggled and strained to raise his arm to silence him. Heaving a breath, and wincing at the ache in his abdomen, he spoke slowly. "It takes courage… to admit… the truth. Let… the boy… speak."

Rajveer nodded at Heera indicating him to proceed.

Heera swallowed a large lump and cleared his throat. "It's a long story…"

He started where he had witnessed Bali being captured and his first encounter with Crook, then being intrigued by Raju's drawing on the slate at the bazaar and seeing him perform with Basanti, and then meeting Maya later with Raju.

Basanti smacked her lips at the mention of her name.

Heera told everyone how he had followed Raju and seen him with Bali and followed him to the bungalow and learned about Benjamin and Raju feeding him his midnight snack.

"I came to the bungalow, like I had told Raju, to meet the Major on the evening the Major had the party. I was sure he wouldn't recognise me. Who'd remember a boy covered in slush and mud? And I did my best to make sure he didn't." Heera told them about how he dressed that day with the turban and kajal. His voice glided smoothly through the stillness in the room, all eyes set on him. "I wanted to get closer to Bali and wanted to be his mahout. The watchman didn't allow me in, and I forced my way in through the side hedge. I saw the Major's wrath over being served rabbit meat and heard some servants speaking about why he was angry. I realised how precious Benjamin was to Crook, just like Bali was to me." Heera recalled the golden cage and velvet cushions inside. He'd never have imagined caging Bali. "Well not quite alike, but still. And an idea struck me. I thought if I took Benjamin I could get the Major to release Bali in exchange for Benjamin."

"How did you manage to steal him with a bungalow full of people?" Maya asked. "It must have been busy with the party."

Heera nodded. "I created a distraction…" Maya screwed her eyes. Heera continued, "…by setting fire to the Major's car."

Everyone in the room gasped.

"That was you?!" Raju hissed.

"I didn't know it was the Major's car then. I just wanted a clear shot at—" he forced himself to say the words aloud. "—at stealing Benjamin." Heera hung his head and said in a lower voice. "To set fire to the Major's car, I used a lighter and that is where it went wrong."

"How did you get Baba's lighter? *Stole* it?" Raju chastised.

"No, I was hiding in a bush when I saw a servant pass by – Ramlal, I think he was. Someone called his name and he left, dropping the lighter on the ground."

Rajveer exclaimed as if he'd realised something. "Ah… Baba, how did Ramlal get your lighter? Did you give it–"

Rajveer nodded halfway through his question.

So, it was *Baba's lighter!* Heera thought and continued. "I seized the opportunity and used it to set the car alight… and finally left it in Crook's dresser before I took Benjamin away." Heera punched a fist into the palm of his other hand in frustration. "I wish I'd been more careful. I didn't expect this… to happen. I didn't mean to put you in trouble."

May he die a rotten death… Raju's words pounded in his ears. He remembered seeing Bali for the first time since he was captured. Injured, helpless and fragile, lying on straw in the enclosure. The sounds and smells of the morning came back too. Bird chirps and the buzzing and the strong, sweet smell of honey.

A sizzle of an idea fizzed, but faded as soon as it had arisen, mangled by the ache in his heart and the bitterness spewing out of Raju's words.

167

"I will be admitting what I've done. It's time to make amends… to get Bali back."

"Child… Crook is ruthless," Rajveer warned.

"Yes… but this is what I had planned all along, to get Bali out. And I think it's time now." Heera's jaw was set. "Tomorrow… I'll tell the Major tomorrow morning, first thing."

Raju stared back with bitter scorn. "How heroic!"

Heera ignored him. His anger was justified.

"You don't think you'll walk into a lion's den and walk out alive, do you?" Maya said, looking at Heera intently.

"I won't." Heera shook his head. "I'll send him a message – written message." He paused as if contemplating something. Then said, "And I can't write so…" He scanned all the faces around him brewing with anxiety and marvel. "Can someone write me a note?"

"What? In English?" Maya asked surprised. "Only that'll make sense to him."

Rajveer shook his head dismissively at Heera who was looking at him hopefully. "Can't write… only… speak," he said effortfully recoiling into his blanket.

"Okay then. Hindi should be good enough. Someone will surely translate it for the Major."

"I know what you need," Maya said keenly.

After a couple of minutes, Heera peered at a makeshift envelope Maya had made him with handmade paper, glued shut with rice glue. On the envelope, Maya had written in Hindi.

To,
Major Crook.
(Urgent – about Benjamin)

Inside it sat a piece of handmade paper with words scribbled on it with ink. Words capable of starting a hurricane.

I have Benjamin. Release the elephant you have caught, if you want Benjamin back. Meet me at the river near the enclosure where you have kept the elephant and bring the animal along. I'll be there.

"Huh! It doesn't even have your name on it. How's that admitting that you did it?" Raju said derisively. "Coward!"

"He's anything but a coward!" Maya looked daggers at Raju. "He saved my—"

"Maya," Heera interjected. "We don't have time for this." He turned to Raju. "I might be in trouble if he finds out too soon. I want to catch him by surprise. Maya, please can you do something for me?"

Maya's father shifted restively. "Please, keep my daughter out of this."

"Appa," Maya glared at her father.

"Don't worry. It's nothing dangerous, I assure you. I only want her to deliver the note to the bungalow tomorrow morning, since I can't risk delivering it."

"But–" Maya's father said.

"Of course," Maya replied with glinting eyes, interrupting her father. "I'll do it, Heera."

"Thank you. But it'll have to be done at first light. Nobody should see you. There's the chowkidar at the front gate. But he'll be sleeping at that hour, most probably. I'll tell you what to do."

Chapter Nineteen

Crook's smug smile in the howdah. Mangal's sneer. Bali's desperate trumpeting. The howling child. The silver anklet. Raju's scowl. The car on fire. Rajveer being kicked brutally. Benjamin in his gold cage. The snakes slithering over Bali's legs. Crook's obnoxious stare.

Heera's mind was a whirlpool of thoughts and memories looping around themselves endlessly. Half-asleep, half-awake, he felt like a fly trapped in a spider-web, desperate for freedom with the unpleasant recollections closing in on him like ravenous spiders.

He heard the front door creak. Vasu had just left for the forest.

Heera felt Benjamin's soft fur against his calf. Cracking his eyes open, he saw the rabbit cuddled up next to him. The thought of the Major made him shudder.

How would he get himself to hold a knife at Benjamin to threaten the Major? There was no way he could have sliced it through the animal. That wasn't who he was. Not even close.

He thought of Maya, hoping she had made it in time to the bungalow to deliver his note.

Bali's hind-leg had healed considerably but he still couldn't walk without dragging it. What if things didn't work out? What if he had to make a run for it with Bali?

What if they were caught? What if Bali was sold?

Heera's mind was a web of what-ifs, innumerable and paralysing.

At least he had to try. It was time for action, he decided.

I will set things right. He set his jaw, grit thumping his chest.

Outside the stark-white bungalow, on a Sheesham tree that stood adjacent to the hedge on the left side of the bungalow, sat Maya, watching her surroundings like a hawk. Dawn hadn't broken yet but the light from the gas-lamps revealed everything that she needed to see.

She had heard the chowkidar snore in his booth, at the front gate that was to the right of the bungalow, just as Heera had said.

Maya felt the heavy mass of the stone in her hands, wrapped with the envelope which had been tied to it with a jute string, making it crinkly. Heera had cleverly rubbed a wax candle over the writing on the envelope, in case it was to land on a wet floor.

She drew a deep breath and hurled the lump at the main door. But she missed.

The stone with the note attached to it had struck the huge ceramic floor vase near the front door, knocking it off its base, splintering it ruthlessly. Maya closed her eyes and held her breath.

The clamour made the chowkidar jump and yell. "Who is it? Who is it?" he shrieked, holding on to his toppling hat, as if speaking to an invisible monster. Stumbling out of his booth with a stick, he scrutinized his surroundings with his puffy eyes half-open. "Must have been a cat," he mumbled, and yawned before retiring back to his booth to drown in slumber.

Peeking through the corner of her eye, Maya saw the front door. It stood undaunted in the dawn, almost as arrogant as its owner. She crossed her fingers for the note to be received.

The increasing daylight hinted her exit and she left for Heera's hut, confident about the delivery of the note.

Around an hour later, Mani appeared in the back

veranda of the bungalow, hands shaking.

"S-Sahib. I found... t-this."

"What is it, Mani?" Crook snapped. "Why are you sounding like a scratched record on a gramophone?"

Crook was seated in a reclining chair, outside his dressing room where a shaft of sunlight had burst in at a convenient angle. His grim eyes were set on the golden cage within the dressing room. Legs resting on the balustrade, Crook wore a blue dressing gown made of silk – the colour concurrent with his mood. It was thrown open at the front revealing his pallid, bare chest to the glaring Indian sun. He appeared to be hoping it would sink deeper into his icy and hopeless heart. Deep furrows of worry ran across his forehead.

"Sahib." Mani held out the severely creased envelope to the Major. "This was at the front door." Mani's 'r's rolled as sharply as ever.

The Major snatched it from him. "Give it here." He peered at it. "What *is* this?" He stretched out the envelope trying to read the text on it. "It's in Hindi. What nonsense is this, Mani?"

Mani shuddered. "Sahib. I-It's for you," he gulped.

"Says *who*?"

"It says, s-sahib." Mani couldn't help his nerves. "It also s-says—"

174

"I'll wallop your behind if you don't speak straight now. What else does it say?"

"It's about Benjamin, sahib."

The Major jerked up from his slouch, his face taut, eyes boring into Mani who didn't dare to meet them. "Where did you find this?" he asked, opening the envelope urgently.

"B-by the front door," Mani replied straining to speak smoothly.

Crook unfurled the crushed note. "Damn! It's in – I can't read this." He held it out to Mani. "Read it. QUICK!" His tone was aggressively commanding.

Mani took the note cautiously. A look at it and the blood drained from his face. His mouth went arid under Crook's sizzling stare.

"What does it say? Speak up, you idiot!"

After Mani had fumbled through the translation of the message, the Major stood up. Tying his dressing robe briskly, he slicked his hair back and let out a hiss of fury. His skin had turned a fiery shade of red-orange from the sun to match his mood.

"Who is this message from?" Crook said slowly, as if considering potential suspects in his mind.

"I don't know, sahib."

"You wouldn't be here if you were that smart. Now get out and get the chowkidar."

Not only the chowkidar, but also the other servants were probed to find out if anyone had been seen around the bungalow, but it was to no avail.

Chapter Twenty

Heera waited for Maya's arrival with bated breath. Ruffling Benjamin's fur, he offered him some grass. "It's been nice knowing you, Benji. I'm sorry you'll be returning to your golden cage." Heera's skin prickled as he looked at the knife he had set aside. He was to hold it at Benjamin's throat later that day, to threaten the Major to release Bali.

There were a couple of other things he had collected in a jute sack: the sap of the tonyoge plant – that grew in his backyard in a goat-skin bag, a hacksaw and a sickle.

He remembered the conversation with Maya the previous night. She had walked him out of her house, nervously clutching the letter she was meant to deliver the next morning. She wasn't anxious about it but about Heera.

"Be careful. You never know how the Major will

react to the note," she had warned.

Heera had nodded to acknowledge her concern but remained silent.

Maya had cleared her throat and said, "So, if I may ask, what is your plan? Are you taking Benji to Bali's enclosure in the forest tomorrow, then?"

"Yes…" Heera had said, as if calculating something. His plan was to wait with Benjamin at the river near the enclosure for the Major and Bali to arrive. Then he would threaten Crook to release Bali for Benjamin. And then it resurfaced; the idea that had fizzled in his mind moments ago. "YES!" Heera stopped on the spot, eyes round and wide.

"Okay, I get it! I just wanted to–" Maya looked at him halfway through her sentence, realising his excitement. "What is it?"

"Nothing. What were you saying?"

"Actually, I wondered what if Crook–" she forced herself to voice the unwelcome possibility aloud. "– doesn't release Bali."

"Then… I will." Heera sounded confident.

"You?" she had asked, bewildered.

"The bees will help me, don't worry. Do you have a hacksaw?"

"Bees?! Hacksaw?!"

"I'll explain. I don't know how I didn't think of this earlier. There are two huge bee hives right there, outside Bali's enclosure."

"So?"

"So? You know how many bees that makes?"

"How many?"

"Many, many, many thousands – if put together they could cover an average carpet." Maya's jaw dropped. "If things don't go as per plan, I'll stone the hive."

"And get stung to death?" Maya looked horrified.

"I've been collecting honey for years; I know how to handle them. Tonyoge plant sap." Heera beamed. "The bees won't attack me if I cover myself with it," he explained, realising Maya's confusion. "It has tranquilising properties. They'll be docile around me."

"And Bali? What about him?"

"Once the bees are all over, the men will flee. I'll reach Bali through the confusion and smear him with plant sap then cut his chain with the hacksaw," Heera said dreamily, imagining Bali walking freely into the forest again. "It's only his ears and eyes that need protection. Then we'll leave. Run. Into the forest," he said, pulling himself back into the present moment.

"That's brilliant. Can I help in any way?" Maya asked, imploring him to say yes.

"It's best you stay away, Maya. I think I've caused enough harm. And I gave my word to your father. I'll be fine on my own."

Maya twisted her mouth to one side in disappointment. "All right." She rolled her eyes. "Appa can be… Anyways, I'll see you tomorrow outside your hut, after I deliver the letter."

There was a rustling sound outside the door. *Must be Maya.*

Heera took Benjamin in his arms and opened the door. The morning was tranquil. The mist hung in the air like a curtain of gloom. A hazy figure shuffled near the neem tree at the side of the hut.

"Maya," he called. "Maya, come out. I know it's you." He walked towards the tree. "Stop playing games, will you?"

He had just about finished his sentence when he was struck on the head with something hard and solid. The forest spun like a top around him. He had seen those eyes before. Gasping, he flopped his arms, letting Benjamin fall away. Then holding his head and barely able to register anything anymore, Heera fell into a black bottomless pit.

Chapter Twenty-One

From behind a tree, Maya watched in horror, as the man threw Heera over his shoulder and carried him away along with Benjamin.

The man was strong-built, and she knew she couldn't fight him. But she had seen his face after he had pulled off the monkey-cap, which only revealed his eyes when he had it on.

A few hours later, Heera gasped for breath. The ache in his head was pounding his skull. He felt his throbbing pulse at his wrists against the rope that dug into his flesh, holding his arms together behind his back. At least his heart was working. His breath came, even if in shallow bursts. He felt reassured. He was alive. Nervously, he ran his tongue over his lips, moistening them, fear burning in his stomach, sharp and acrid.

Muffled sounds somewhere in the distance faded in and out.

He wondered where he was, the darkness shrouding him. He opened his mouth to swallow air and felt it on his arid lips. It smelled of earth and dung and of something very sweet. *Honey!*

As if confirming his judgement, a trumpeting alerted him. *Bali!*

He was at the enclosure in the forest, just as he had judged. Probably inside one of the village men's makeshift housings, he thought.

Light teased in through a crack in the wooden window shutter somewhere above him. When he squinted to look at it, the hurt in his head nipped, making him cringe in pain.

Benjamin… Bali… Crook. The eyes of the attacker. Everything came gushing back with a bang.

Heera struggled into a sitting position and tried to look around in the frail light.

They took him. Benjamin. Oh no.

His heart sank to his heels. His plan had fallen apart even before he had started to execute it. How would he ever get the Major to release Bali? Had he failed? Failed Bali?

A tear ran down his cheek stinging his bruised lips.

Outside, he heard horse hooves slowing to a halt. A door was wrenched open somewhere behind him and he instinctively twisted in the sitting position to look. The light bursting in through the door hurt his eyes causing his pupils to constrict.

A man stood in the door, the sunlight behind him turning him into a dark silhouette.

"Hope you've had a good sleep, boy."

The voice was instantly recognisable. Heera's breath faltered.

It was Mangal.

Heera was lifted to his feet.

Light had flooded the room enough for Heera to look into Mangal's eyes. They matched his attacker's.

"Where's Benjamin? It was you, wasn't it?" Heera asked, scowling.

"You still doubt it?" Mangal sneered. "There's no hurry, is there? You'll find out soon, about Benjamin."

Mangal grabbed Heera by his neck and the tufts of his shorter hair, forcing him roughly towards the door. A sharp shove in his lower back caused Heera to stumble across the threshold and fall clumsily to the ground, tasting earth on his lips.

Bali let out a furious trumpet. Chains around his legs clanked violently with every tug. He had caught Heera's scent.

It's okay, Bali. Calm down.

Steel-capped boots, at eye-level, strode towards him. Heera craned his neck upwards to look at stony, grey eyes slatted yellow like a snake's, drilling into him. Crook stood tall with Benjamin in his arms. Heera hadn't ever been this close to him.

Bali's enclosure lay a few yards behind Crook and the room where Heera was held was behind him.

Crook slid the tip of his shoe under Heera's chin, holding it up at a sore angle. "You're brave, I have to say." His lips twisted briefly into a smile as empty as a carcass. "But you're stupid… utterly foolish. What made you think you could get away with this?" His voice was low, cold, and full of menace. Contemptuously, he chucked a piece of crushed paper at Heera. It landed next to his face.

Crook lifted Benjamin to his face and rubbed his nose against the rabbit's. "My Benji," he crooned. The rabbit dangled from his arms like a limp, lifeless toy. Crook looked at Mangal. "Ask this guttersnipe," he commanded. "Has he any idea how much comfort Benji is used to? He has missed his *golden* home, his luxuries, his midnight snacks. He's no longer himself. Ask him."

"Yes, sahib," Mangal replied, hands held together in front of his body, slightly flustered by the Major's whims.

When Mangal had finished translating the Major's words to Heera, Crook put Benjamin down. The rabbit scurried over to Heera's head and licked his temple with his warm, wet tongue.

"Traitor!" the Major bellowed. He took his foot out from under Heera's chin and, before Heera could feel the relief, Crook thrust it with such force at Benjamin that he sent him spiralling several feet away.

Heera uttered a small howl, wriggling helplessly to the motionless pile of white fluff.

Mangal swallowed nervously at the Major's reaction.

Heera turned his eyes away from Benjamin to the crushed ball of paper lying next to his face. Initially it was a blur through his glazed eyes, but soon, through the wrinkles, he recognised Maya's handwriting. The Major had received the note.

Crook was aware that *he* had taken Benjamin. Not Baba. Even though he wondered how, a part of him was relieved. Raju and his Baba would have their home back soon. He had corrected the damage he had caused.

"Up. Up, you little runt," Crook shouted.

Mangal seized Heera and lifted him to his feet, holding his neck and arms. Heera cried in pain.

"A little surprise for you," Crook said, his tone brimming with bitter sarcasm, and Mangal translating with equal amounts of it.

Another man walked in, nudging his prisoner forward by the shoulder.

"Ma. No," Heera gasped, digging his nails into

185

his palms till they hurt. "Let her go." His throat felt as dry as dust.

"Heera, my child. Are you okay?" Vasu cried, struggling against her captor's vice-like grip. She looked at Bali and gasped. "Bali!" she whispered in amazement.

"How emotional!" Mangal mocked.

"Good insurance, eh? In case you start off with your monkey-tricks again!" The Major cackled.

Mangal scratched his head, wondering what Crook had meant by insurance. "Good idea, sahib," he flattered, cocking his head from side to side.

Crook glowered at him. "Shut up and tell him what I said. He causes me any more trouble and he'll lose his mother."

"Sahib is saying, any trouble you cause, and you'll lose your mother," Mangal warned. "If there's any trace of intelligence in you, you'll forget all about your elephant."

"What are you looking at?" Crook asked Vasu's captor. "Lock that woman away."

Mangal signalled at Vasu's captor. "Oye! Throw her in there."

"Ma isn't a part of this. Let her go," Heera pleaded.

"Leave my son. Please. Heera…" Vasu's voice trailed off as she was dragged away and shut inside the room Heera had been in earlier. A man bolted the door shut and left a huge lock hanging from the bolt.

Bali's trumpet went off again in the background.

Hotly, Heera spat at the Major.

Crook strode towards Heera, his eyes bulging and livid and his lips drawn back in a hideous sneer. He turned to glance at Bali and then back at Heera, "He's as impertinent a beast… as *you*." His right eye twitched as he spoke. "You haven't learned how to behave since we first met, have you?" Heera breathed in his cologne; overpowering and savagely sharp, like its wearer.

Mangal slapped the back of Heera's head. "Sahib knows who you are. I told him," he said smugly. "That you were the waif he met in the forest while catching that elephant, the one who had been disrespectful to him. Remember?" He shook Heera by his hair. "You think you're too smart, haan? Think I wouldn't recognise you?"

Bali bellowed, yanking at the chains.

"Give that boisterous animal a good whacking," Crook yelled.

"Don't, sahib —" An old man hobbled over to Crook's side. He had been passive until then but couldn't hold himself back anymore. "He's not dangerous – the elephant – only disturbed." Heera recognised him. It was Hariya.

"Don't you dare tell me what to do," Crook

snapped.

Two men, with bamboo sticks taller than themselves, advanced towards Bali. Clenching his teeth, the first one jabbed his stick into Bali's flank while the other did the same below his ears.

Bali winced with pain and let out a screeching trumpet that shook the ground.

"NOOOO," Heera cried. He was a spitting bundle of rage, nostrils flaring like an angry bull. "PLEASE STOP!" Mangal tugged harder at his hair, and he groaned in pain.

Hariya flashed an apologetic look at Heera. To Heera, however, he was only a hazy outline from behind the veil of tears.

The men continued striking Bali. The menacing thuds and Bali's roars echoed in Heera's ears, gashing his soul.

"BALI!" Heera screamed, but soon the strength drained from his voice. "Please stop hitting him. Do what you like with me but let him go. I beg you. I'll never come back. Just stop hitting him."

"Aha! Someone's learning to behave now!" Mangal sneered.

"What did he say?" Crook asked.

"Sahib. He says he'll never come back if we stop hitting the elephant."

Crook gave an icy-cold hoot of laughter.

"Stop!" he barked at the men prodding at Bali.

"Leave the animal."

Relief washed over Heera and his body relaxed, his legs staggering under his own weight.

"I'm not trusting any word from that stray," Crook said. Mangal opened his mouth to say something, but Crook dismissed him with an impatient wave of his hand. "Take him away. Hang him in the forest. Leave him to be preyed on."

Soon, a sack was thrown over Heera's head and tied around his neck with a rope.

Heera was walked into the forest. He didn't know what direction and he couldn't count his steps because he didn't know how to count beyond four. All he had was a sense of time. They had walked for about half an hour before he was tied to a tree. The light had significantly reduced.

How did you know? he wanted to ask Mangal, but he couldn't speak through the cloth gagging his mouth.

As if answering his question, Mangal spoke. "You think I wouldn't recognise you? It was all too strange, the instant bond between you and the animal. I knew there was more to it. And it was confirmed after you called him Bali. It was the same name you shouted out in the forest that day. The day Bali was caught. 'Let my friend go. Let Bali go,'" Mangal teased.

Heera felt like an idiot.

"You actually took Benjamin?" Mangal continued, enjoying the one-way conversation. "I knew following you would lead me to more."

Heera swore mentally. He had been followed, after all. It wasn't his imagination. How could he have been so reckless?

Chapter Twenty-Two

It was night. That was all Heera could make out through the sack covering his head: the lack of sunlight. The cricket song flooding the night gave it away too. There was a flutter of wings, and he imagined the bats flitting past in the moonlight.

He struggled to breathe.

The blood gushing to his head made him dizzy. His face was puffy and flushed. It was more than an hour since he had been hung upside down from a tree branch. Every inch of his body was raw from gravity acting upon it, stretching it taut as a tripwire.

Judging by the rustling of the leaves in the gentle night breeze, he couldn't have been more than a few feet above the ground.

He felt a warm trickle running up his arm. And instantly realised it was blood. *His* blood.

The flesh on his wrist burned where the rope had

cut through it causing his wounds to bleed. He knew that the scent of his oozing blood would attract a predator, sooner than later.

As soon as the thought came to him, he heard a growling far away somewhere. His hair stood on end. Minutes later, the sound of footfalls over leaves followed. Terror knotted his stomach, seeping through his veins and spreading bile to the back of his throat. The air around him quivered with anticipation.

The footfalls neared. Soon it would be all over, he thought. The thought of his mother and of how she would cope without him caused a sob to well up in his throat and he pressed his lips together to try and smother it. He thought of Bali. *Forgive me, dost.*

A presence neared, closer than ever. All his instincts screamed at him to run. But how could he? He could only hope for it to be as painless as possible. He braced himself, screwing his eyes shut, and hoped it would end soon.

Something clutched his neck. He froze. Then there was a tugging and tearing at his collar. This was it!

From behind his closed eyelids, he sensed light. Was that the glow of the spirits of his ancestors Ma had always talked about? He thought of the tattoo on his body. They would surely recognise him.

He heard the rasping of the jute sack as it was

torn away from his face. He gulped air and let out a strangled wail.

"Heera," a familiar voice rang in his ears. "It's me, Maya. Are you okay?"

Maya's face glowed orange in the flames of the fire-torch she held.

Heera squinted at her face, relief swathing him like a warm blanket.

"We're here to get you," Maya assured him.

We? Upside down, Heera struggled to identify the person next to him, turned into a dark shadow by the flaming torch in Maya's hands.

"Raju and me," she said.

Raju?!

He heard a swishing noise on the tree he was hung from. If the two of them were here, who was on the tree? he wondered.

There was a SNAP and the next moment he came crashing down.

Although Maya had cushioned his fall by cradling his head, the twigs and pebbles on the ground nipped his already tender body. At least he was free. He was grateful. He sat up gradually, holding onto his head. The blood rushing back to the rest of his body made him light-headed.

A macaque dropped to the ground beside him, making him jump. It was Basanti.

Raju clicked his tongue and held out his hand to

the macaque, as if demanding something. Basanti placed a small knife into his palm. Raju held out a guava in return. "Good girl, Basanti." Basanti smacked her lips, took the guava and crouched quietly beside Raju, biting into it.

"Did she–? She's clever," Heera mumbled weakly, his surprise dampened by the ache in his body.

"No doubt!" Raju said proudly. He held out a goat-skin bag full of water.

Heera eagerly put it to his lips, relishing every precious drop of invigorating coolness. It was revitalising bliss.

"Thank you." Heera looked at Maya and then at Raju who nodded shortly.

"No problem," Raju replied.

"We don't have much time," Maya spoke urgently. "They're taking Bali away at dawn."

"What? Where to?" Heera jerked to his feet, forgetting all his physical pain.

"To Gazalpur. For an auction."

"Auction? What's an auction?"

"Where they sell things… and animals too. I heard the men. Let's go now. I'll tell you on the way."

Heera looked around him, already fired up. Although he had never been in the forest at this hour, it wasn't alien to him. The moon washed the jungle in a gentle light. He looked up. "It's a full moon," he declared. "We shouldn't have trouble seeing. But we should keep the fire-torch to keep predators away."

"Predators?! I thought they slept at night," Maya stammered.

"We'll be fine with the torch as long as you have enough fuel to keep it going."

"We do," Raju said. He patted a little cloth bag thrown across his body.

"Good." Heera nodded at Raju. "Most animals don't hurt unless disturbed," he reassured Maya. "Which way did you come?"

"Er – that way… I think." Maya pointed to the east.

A patch of sky above them was speckled with stars, sprinkled around like diamond dust on black velvet.

"No. I think it's that way," Raju insisted. "We changed direction. I remember."

"Are you sure?" Heera asked, studying the confusion on their faces.

"Okay, let's start walking at least," Raju suggested.

"And what if we head in the wrong direction?" Maya asked.

"We didn't walk too much to get here. I have a sense of roughly how long we took, so we shouldn't be very far from the enclosure. If we're heading in the wrong direction, I'll know since it'll be dawn soon and I'll be able to tell where we are when the sky is lighter."

"Fine. Listen to him then." Maya nudged Raju. "At least you won't blame me if we're heading in the wrong direction."

"Maya," Heera said, trying to placate her. "We'll figure that out later. First, we need a plan."

"Fine," Maya grimaced and held out a sack of stuff to Heera. "Here you go."

"How did you get this?" Heera beamed at her, instantly recognising it. It was the sack that contained the things he set aside to take along to the enclosure with Benjamin. It had the goat-skin bag full of tonyoge plant sap, a hacksaw and a sickle. "How did you—"

"I was right there when Mangal attacked you and took Benjamin. I saw everything."

"Really? Where?"

"I watched from behind a tree not far from your hut. Had I come minutes earlier, I would have been there when he hit you. When he took you, I went into the hut and saw this sack. You mentioned the bees and the plant sap last night so I brought it along."

"You don't know how grateful I am." Heera smiled. Maya smiled widely, to acknowledge his gratitude, dimples sinking deeper into her cheeks. "This makes things so much easier." He rummaged through the sack, checking the contents.

"I went to fetch Raju," Maya continued, looking at Raju. "I told him what had happened, secretively of course, or else Appa would have locked me up before I even reached you."

Heera looked at Raju with an expression that said something like, *I didn't expect you'd come.*

"I'm sorry for yesterday," Raju said in a matter-of-fact way. "I was—"

Heera waved off the apology. "It's okay. I would have probably done the same." He spoke looking at Basanti and then flicked his eyes at Raju. "And now that the Major knows who took Benji, you should have your home back." Raju nodded graciously. Heera looked at Maya. "Thank you for delivering that note for me."

"It's okay. Don't worry about it. But… why did he kick Benji? The Major, I mean… What kind of a man does that?" Maya asked.

"You saw that?"

"Yes, we were watching you from the top of a tree nearby."

"You think only you can follow people?" Raju winked.

"That was clever," Heera said and smiled. "I think Crook didn't like Benji licking me. That's the way rabbits express love. The man is crazy."

"Clearly!" Maya said. "We also followed you and Mangal into the forest. But we stayed back a bit, to listen for any important information, and to wait for Crook to depart before we came down from the tree. And we also lost our way slightly trying to keep our distance from Mangal and you. And finally, we managed to get to you."

Heera listened, his eyes glistening with admiration. "Honestly, thanks for coming for me. I was sure I'd be eaten alive out here. You've both risked so much for me."

There was a moment of awkward silence between the three, that Maya broke.

"Aren't you too solemn for a jungle boy?" she chuckled, dimples burrowing into her cheeks. "I only came to have an adventure. Appa would never let me," she rolled her eyes and added, "So I seized my chance. Anyways, let's focus on the plan now."

"Yeah. The idea I had with the bees should still work, but I'm not sure if we have enough sap for us all. And, they've also locked up Ma. They've put her in a room with a huge lock on the door."

Basanti's noisy chomping on the guava attracted Heera's attention. Something clicked in his head.

"Wait! Doesn't she open locks? Basanti?" he asked, his mind a jumble of calculations.

"Yes of course. How did… you know?" Raju

asked puzzled.

"I've seen you perform on the streets. You're quite good." Raju waved away the compliment.

"Maya, do you have a hair pin?" Heera asked.

"Should do." Maya felt around her head. "Yup, two."

"That'll do, won't it?" Heera looked at Raju who nodded back. "Great!"

"You can use the plant sap for yourself and Bali," Raju said. "I'll be fine. I've been bitten before by bees and have survived it so there's no reason I can't again."

Maya's face crumpled with anxiety.

"We'll all use it," Heera said firmly, looking at Maya. "But only on our faces. The rest of our bodies should be okay without it. And I'll save some for Bali around his eyes and a little under his ears. Those are the most sensitive areas."

Maya's face relaxed.

Chapter Twenty-Three

"You said you heard the men?" Heera asked Maya, speaking through mouthfuls of guava. "What did they say?"

"I only heard an old man, just after Mangal had taken you away. The man had a thick white moustache."

"Must be Hariya," Heera said. "What did he say?"

"He told the others that it was as per Crook's orders that they had to leave for Gazalpur with Bali just after sunrise."

"Did he say if Crook was coming too?"

"Not that I remember. Although, I doubt he will. He has a motor car to get there."

"Not anymore," Raju said. "After Heera set fire to it."

Maya chuckled. "Oh yes! But he can always use his horse then. Why would he stress himself with a slow journey with an elephant?"

"Hmm… makes sense," Heera said, gorging down the last bite of fruit and licking the sweetness off his fingertips. "So, here is what we do. When we get there, the men are likely to be awake given that they're taking Bali away to Gazalpur. I know where the bee hives are, so I'll creep in and strike them with a rock. The bees will swarm the place and I'll head to Bali with Maya, in the mayhem. Maya, you can start hacking the chain with the hacksaw while I smear Bali's face with plant sap. Then I can pick up from where you leave off, and cut him free. In the meanwhile, Raju can get Basanti to open the lock to the room where Ma is. I'll point to it once we get there. Raju, you can keep the torch to keep the bees away from Ma and Basanti. And you already have a knife for self-defence."

"Uh, yes, but there's one problem. Basanti may panic on seeing the bees."

"In that case," Heera said thoughtfully. "You'll have to get to Ma first, that is before I strike the hive. For that, we'll need to distract the men." Heera looked at Maya and narrowed his eyes.

"What is it?" Maya asked suspiciously.

"Nobody would suspect a weeping girl," Heera said.

Maya's eyes widened, then her forehead shrivelled with a frown. "Weep? What for?"

"For seeing a… tiger… near somewhere. Just run to the men for help. Create a commotion. Your crying is supposed to lure them in. So, feel free to howl your lungs out. But don't overdo it. Am sure you'll do well."

"Sure. Whatever makes you think I'm good at it?" Maya said with her hands on her hips.

Heera was already scanning the ground below for a small twig. Spotting one, he picked it up and then sat down on his haunches. He cleared a small area of forest floor of leaves to reveal the soil below then started to etch a map into the soil with his twig.

"This is roughly how the place looks. We'll go to them from behind the enclosure," he said, pointing to Bali's enclosure on his map, "so that they're drawn away from the room that holds Ma." He pointed at the small square on the ground that represented the room.

"Who's we?" Maya asked.

"I'll come with you," Heera replied. "I can mimic tiger growls quite well. It'll help in convincing the men." Maya peered back in approbation. "Then," Heera continued, "Raju, and Basanti will creep in at the back and have a go at the lock. Once the men start assembling at the back of the enclosure, due to your *false* tiger alarm, I'll get back to Raju, and after

Ma is out, I'll strike the hives and go to Bali. Maya, once I leave your side, just make sure you come to the enclosure on the pretext of being terrified by the tiger. Raju, you can stay with Ma and keep her safe."

The trio walked through patches of misty moonlight shining through the gaps in the trees. They had chosen to walk in Raju's suggested direction.

Heera wondered what the future held. It looked optimistic but uncertain.

"I'm glad to have the help of you two. Couldn't have dreamt of this on my own. Although you shouldn't be here without telling your father. Same for Raju," Heera said.

"Don't worry. Raju's Baba knows about this."

"He does?"

"Yes. It was he who encouraged Raju to help you out. He thought you were very brave to speak the truth." Flushed, Heera looked away from Maya. "In fact, he said he'd handle my father too if I chose to go. I was going to help you anyway."

"Is he better now?"

"Getting there, I suppose. It's hard to tell after a certain age."

Heera's face fell. "It's all my fault. I've been so careless about everything lately."

"It's okay."

"No, it's not. Mangal had been stalking me for

days. How could I have not noticed?" Heera punched a fist in the air.

"Happens to the best of us," Maya reassured him.

Raju was walking ahead, leading the way with the torch in one hand and with Basanti on a lead in the other.

"Mangal recognised me from the first time he saw me in the jungle, when–" Heera stopped mid-sentence, abandoning his words. Distracted. And listened to the silence around him.

"What is it?" Maya asked, her face twisting with worry. "A predator?"

Heera put a finger to his lips. His forehead wrinkled with deep concentration, and he closed his eyes to focus. Then losing the lines on his forehead, he said softly, "Can you hear that?" His face looked unusually light and serene in the pallid beam of the moonlight.

"Hear *what*?" Maya asked, her desperation heightening.

Raju walked towards them, crushing leaves under his feet.

"Shh! Just listen," Heera whispered.

Buried deep within the cricket song, the whispers of the night breeze and the occasional scuttling sounds of hedgehogs foraging around, was the faint bubbling sound of a stream.

"The river," Heera said.

"The river?" Raju and Maya chorused.

"It's there. We're not far." Heera pointed ahead. "We're heading towards it. Which means that we're heading in the wrong direction."

"Told you," Maya jumped in. She wiggled her thumb at Raju, teasing him. "I knew I was right."

Raju tried to ignore her.

"So which way do we go, then?"

"The enclosure is not far from the river, and I don't remember crossing the river when Mangal got me here. However, the river lies behind that whole area which means we have to head in the opposite direction."

"You aren't right, either," Raju told Maya, throwing her a grimace.

Maya rolled her eyes at him.

"Let's walk that way." Heera looked at the sky. It had turned lighter. "Soon I'll be able to climb a tall tree and see if we can spot the river."

Chapter Twenty-Four

As they walked through the forest, the trees cast eerie shapes and shadows in the light of the fire-torch.

Soon the first calls of the dawn chorus echoed across the forest, the soft light replacing the damp gloom of the night. The blanket of fog started to lift.

Heera scrambled up a tree effortlessly, shaking dew drops off the laden leaves. Clinging dew bent the shivering blades of grass below, making it look like a field of liquid diamonds.

Peering around from the treetop, Heera took a swig of the morning air. A rim of pale pink had formed on the eastern horizon. The canopies of trees stretched around him like a gigantic bushy carpet. And beyond it, behind them, in the distance, he could see the river, a huge fabric of shimmering silver. He climbed back down.

"We're on the right path," he declared.

Before Maya and Raju could react, a trumpeting sound cut through the dawn.

Bali! Heera's heart both leaped and sank at the same time.

He hurried along while the two followed.

When they were closer, sounds of men rushing around faded in. Heera peeked out from the dense undergrowth. They'd reached the back of the make-do shelters that were around a hundred yards away. From where they were, Bali's enclosure was hidden from view.

"We'll have to make our way to the back of the enclosure. Once we get there, I'll tell you when and then you cry out as loud as you can, 'Tiger! Tiger!'"

Maya's lips stretched into a horizontal line across her face. "But what if they ask me what I was doing here at this hour?"

"I doubt they'll ask you anything after hearing you've seen a *tiger* skulking nearby."

"But what if?" Maya's tone was adamant, and Heera knew there was no point trying to win an argument with her.

"Make something up. Say you came to peel cinnamon bark." Maya nodded, satisfied with the answer, and heaved a breath seeking composure.

"Point away from the enclosure into the forest

on the other side to show them where you saw the tiger. That way, we drive the men away from the enclosure and away from Raju and Basanti, so that they can rescue Ma."

"Oh, give me the hair pins," Raju said.

Maya quickly felt her hair and slid the pins out carefully.

"Raju, I'll try to be back as soon as possible. But there's no guarantee. Ma is in there." Heera pointed to the shelters in front of them. "It's the one in the middle. If I can't get here in time, I'll make the hooting sound of an owl once we draw the men to the back of the enclosure. Look out for this signal…" Heera let out a hoot that sounded uncannily like an owl.

Raju looked astounded.

"I'll do this twice. When you hear this you can go ahead even if I can't get to you."

"How do you do that?" Maya asked, amusement glinting in her eyes.

"I don't know. I just do." Heera looked at the ground, awkward at the praise. "I've lived in the forest long enough, I guess." He quickly moved on. "I think we're too far back right now." He peered ahead. "Why don't you go hide behind that huge rock near the shelters?" He looked at the fire-torch in Raju's hand. "Will this last long enough?"

"Yes, I tied on some more rags dipped in

kerosene, while you were up that tree."

"That's good. The torch will help you defend yourself against the men and the bees too."

Raju smiled and held the torch high. "Jai Bajrang Bali!" he said theatrically.

Heera caught a glimpse of the tattoo on the inside of his arm again. His smile went out instantaneously like a candle in the wind, his countenance a web of confusion and daze.

"What is it?" Raju asked.

"N-nothing. Give me your palm."

"Why?" Raju asked.

"Quick. You need to put on some plant sap. Rub some on your face."

He reached into his sack and pulled out the goat-skin bag with the tonyoge plant sap in it. It poured out onto Raju's palm in uneven lumps like jelly, and smelled earthy and green like the forest.

After Raju had coated his face and neck with plant sap, Heera and Maya did the same.

"It'll look like sweat to the men. Pretend you are out of breath from running away from the tiger," Heera explained. Maya smiled. "Now let's go." Heera tucked the goat-skin bag into his sack and hurried with Maya to the back of the enclosure.

Picking up a few chunky stones on his way, Heera put them into the sack he had on his shoulder. Reaching the undergrowth, they sat low behind some bushes. From there they could see two majestic white bulls tied to a two-wheeled bullock cart that was being loaded with straw and supplies for the journey. There was only one man loading the straw. Heera hadn't seen him earlier.

"Good, we can test this now," Heera whispered.

Maya looked at him bewildered. "What are you doing?"

Heera cupped his hands around his mouth and made a guttural growling sound like a predator.

The man was bent low over the bundle of straw, ready to haul it onto the cart. He didn't move for a moment, but soon he resumed his activity.

"Goodness. What else can you do? I'd have fallen for that." Maya chuckled softly. "But am I not supposed to go there before you start growling like a tiger?"

"What's the point if they can't hear it? I'm making sure we're at a good distance, so they can hear the growls and, when you mention a tiger, they actually believe you." Heera looked at a sheesham tree closer to the enclosure. "You wait here. I'll have to go there. Then, even if they come here looking for the tiger, they won't see me. If this works, I'll throw a stone near you to signal you to step out. Start screaming and then go running to him."

Maya nodded, not very confident about herself. Heera carefully made his way up the tree and positioned himself on a branch densely shrouded with leaves.

Maya sat apprehensively in the bushes waiting for the cue.

Again, cupping his hands around his mouth, Heera made a snarling sound. This time, the man jumped in his skin and glanced around nervously. One of the bulls moved restively, striking its hooves on the ground.

"Brilliant," Heera mumbled. "This is working."

The man looked alarmed. He wiped the sweat off his brow and turned his back to Heera to face another man who was approaching him. Heera hadn't seen this man either. The two men exchanged words that were inaudible to him. However, the few edgy glances they threw around were enough to convey the message: they suspected a lurking predator.

It was time to strike when the iron was hot. Heera flung a stone towards Maya. It landed a foot away from her.

Maya cleared her throat and let out a piercing scream.

The men were alarmed. One of them almost fell and held onto his turban.

"Tiger! Tiger!" Maya ran out of the bushes, panting hard. "Help, help!"

"What? Where?" one of them asked.

Heera let out another growl. Maya screamed.

"It's just there. I saw it. At least ten feet long and paws as big as your face."

One of the men ran back towards the shelters. "Let's get the others."

The other man shouted and ran to the bulls. "Help! My bulls! They're in danger. Hurrrrr!" He patted the bulls. "We need to get them out of here."

"Oye! What's going on?" Mangal's burly body appeared on hearing the confusion. His head was held high and his chest stuck out. "Who's this girl?"

Heera bit his lip in vehemence, his crown still sore from the blow. This man had almost killed him and virtually destroyed his chances of freeing Bali.

A shiver danced down Maya's spine on seeing Mangal. She'd seen how pitiless he had been to Heera and in taking Benjamin away.

"T-tiger – I saw it there – Please save me." Maya ran to Mangal's side. "I don't want to be eaten. Please, please, do something." Stroking his ego would help, she thought.

"Calm down, girl. Nothing will happen while I'm here," Mangal replied in his husky voice. "Get your sticks, everyone." He turned to one of the two men who had been standing next to the bulls. "Krishna, get the others. Quick. And their sticks."

The plan was working, and Heera had begun to enjoy himself. He growled like a tiger again. This

212

time for Mangal.

Mangal's eyes widened, and his hefty frame pivoted on his heels to scan his surroundings.

A commotion followed and soon a gang gathered behind him with sticks.

"There's a tiger lurking around. We need to be vigilant," Mangal addressed the men. "We don't want the beast to disrupt our plans. We should be able to leave safely with the elephant so let's drive it away." Mangal thudded his stick on the ground.

Heera scanned the crowd from the tree top. There were about five men in total including Mangal but excluding Hariya who wasn't present in the crowd. Obviously the additional two men had been hired for the journey. Heera hoped that there weren't many more in the shelters, although the possibility of Hariya being there was likely. It wasn't the ideal time for him to go to Raju since the men had started to scatter.

Raju, this is for you.

OOH-OOOH-OOOOH-OOOO

OOH-OOOH-OOOOH-OOOO

Heera crossed his fingers and hoped for Raju to pick up the signal.

Chapter Twenty-Five

Raju's hair stood on end listening to Heera's owl's hoot. He clenched his fist and felt the hairpins in his palm. It was time to act. Now.

"Come on, Basanti," he said, tucking the hair pins into the cloth belt at his waist and peering out from behind the rock where they had been hiding.

Keeping his head low and holding on to the torch, Raju creeped towards the shelters. He held onto Basanti's lead, guiding her along.

They were at the back wall of one of the shelters. It was made of bamboo and plastered with mud and dung. The door was ajar. Raju held his breath and peeped in. It was empty. He heaved a sigh of relief.

Peeping from behind the wall of this shelter, he could see only one other shelter in front. So, he went to the other side and peeped from the other end. A similar shelter stood closer than the one he had seen from the other side.

All three shelters made a kind of triangle, he realised, with each shelter at an apex of the triangle. The one in front was closest to the enclosure and blocked his view of Bali in the enclosure. The one behind it, which had Vasu in it, was leftmost and out of line with the other two shelters. It had a huge pile of straw sitting next to it.

He couldn't help but smell the sweetness floating in the air and spotted the hives hanging from a huge tree between the enclosure and the shelters. Those were the hives Heera had mentioned earlier, he realised.

Raju had to get to the shelter ahead. Luckily the door was facing them and he could see the lock on it. He decided it was probably better letting Basanti go ahead first. Nobody would suspect a macaque.

Swapping hands to hold the torch, he reached his cloth belt with his free hand to pull out a jamun and a hair pin.

"Come on, Basanti," he whispered, stroking the macaque's head, and held out a jamun. Basanti opened and shut her mouth rapidly and took the jamun. Eating it in one bite, she spat the seed out and licked her lips, now bright purple from the fruit's pulp. "You'll get more. But first, show me your magic." Raju held out the hair pin. "There, open that lock." He pointed at the lock ahead. Basanti looked attentively at him and soon her gaze shifted to the lock. She knew what had been asked of her and sprang towards the lock with the hair pin.

Raju prayed for nobody to notice her. Basanti was proficient at this. There was no doubt she could do this, he told himself. He saw Basanti at the door, cocking her head and scrutinising the lock dangling above her head from the bolt on the door.

Inserting the pin into the plug of the padlock, Basanti felt around as if listening to the clicks in it. She didn't look alarmed. Raju decided it was safe for him to proceed.

Watching his surroundings, he quickly tiptoed to the second shelter behind Basanti, torch in hand.

Basanti fiddled around for minutes and nothing happened.

Raju's brow had started to bead up with perspiration. "What's wrong? Hurry up, Basanti. Good girl."

There was a shuffling sound from inside the room. Raju put his ear to the door.

"Who is it?" a weak female voice asked.

Raju hesitated, then spoke close to the door. "Are you Heera's mother? I'm Raju, Heera's dost."

At the back of the enclosure, the men had started searching for the tiger. Heera sat where he was and growled occasionally and threw an occasional rock into the undergrowth to distract the men.

Maya pointed in random directions, saying that she saw the tiger. She stepped towards the front of the enclosure gradually.

The hair pin snapped into two and a part of it fell to the ground. Thankfully, Maya had given him two. But the half of the first pin was jutting out of the lock.

Raju struggled to pull it out with one hand, the other occupied with the torch.

"Goodness! Why do things go wrong when they absolutely shouldn't?" he complained.

Holding the torch as upright and as steady as he could, he crouched low until he was face to face with the lock. He angled his face and managed to grip the part of the hair pin sticking out of the lock with his molars. Finally, he got a grip on it and, with a mighty heave, he yanked it out.

"Phew!" Air left his lungs with the vigour of respite. "Here." He gave Basanti another jamun. Basanti ate the fruit eagerly. "Now, open the lock, hurry up, girl!" Raju pulled the second pin out and gave it to Basanti. She inserted the new hair pin into the lock.

Come on, come on. Raju's heart was pacing. The seconds stretched out into an eternity.

CLICK, CLICK.

And the lock fell open.

Raju inhaled deeply.

Basanti took the lock out of the bolt and threw it to the ground.

"Good girl. Well done, Basanti." Raju slid open the bolt. Then he reached down to his belt to fetch a jamun for Basanti. But there was something wrong with her.

She was crouched low and baring her teeth instead of smacking her lips in anticipation of the prize.

"What's wrong?" he said, as a firm hand landed on his shoulder from behind. He froze, tasting bile.

"What's going on here?" It was one of the men who had come back to fetch his stick and spotted them.

Raju turned, his stomach churning with horror.

Basanti put her head down, and drew her ears back and let out a bark, sensing a threat.

The man gripped Raju by his collar. "What were you up to, little rogue?" He shook Raju's little frame pugnaciously.

The fire-torch fell from Raju's hands and rolled away.

The two spun around, swapping sides. The man's back was now at the door while Raju was now facing it, breathless, wide-eyed and dazed.

Moments later, a cracking noise rang in Raju's

ears. He wheezed. The man's hands around his collar went limp, his eyes rolled back, and he fell to the ground.

Dizzy with shock, Raju looked up from the man prone to a small-framed woman facing him.

Vasu looked worn out but the warmth in her eyes and the soft smile on her face was contagious.

Raju relaxed.

Vasu held the round rim of the earthen pot, while the rest of it lay shattered next to the man on the ground.

"You're Heera's friend?" she asked, casting the rim away and dusting her hands together, wiping them on her saree.

"Y-yes."

"Thank you, son. Where is Heera?" Her face creased with worry.

"I should thank *you* for knocking him out." Raju looked down at the man.

"Where is Heera?" she asked again. "Did he send you here?" Then, without warning, her eyes darted to something behind Raju. And her expression rapidly changed to one of horror.

A waft of hot air caught Raju's back. He spun around to follow Vasu's gaze, and gasped.

Smouldering fire licked the bottom of the heap of straw like a hungry kitten with a saucer of milk, crackling, playful and gentle at first, before spiralling into a gigantic monster.

NO. NO. NO!!! Raju threw his hands to his head.

Basanti jumped towards Raju's feet. Crouching low, she screamed.

The torch had rolled into the heap setting the straw ablaze. And this was going to attract the attention of everyone at the enclosure.

Before they could do anything, the fire flared and leaped spitting out sparks like a fountain spraying water. Plumes of grey-black smoke wound around the heap like a hungry serpent rising to the skies.

Chapter Twenty-Six

Bali sensed the fire, or the heat, and started to rumble in fright.

Raju ran to the heap of burning straw. The length of the torch was still visible, sticking out from the pile. Only its burning mouth was in contact with the blaze. He picked it up. The heat scorched his body.

"Quick. Let's go. That way," he pointed to the rock they had been hiding behind and darted towards it, pulling Basanti by the lead. Vasu followed.

When they reached the third shelter farthest from the enclosure, a figure stepped out from behind it.

Raju jumped in his skin. "Heera!" he gasped. "You gave me a fright. How did you get here?"

"The men will be here soon. They were out searching for the tiger, but some have been alarmed by the rising smoke. I managed to dodge their attention and came to check on you all." He saw his mother. "Ma!"

"Heera!" Vasu ran to Heera and wrapped him in her arms.

"Are you okay, Ma?" Heera asked. His eyes whizzed past her to the fire behind her. "How did that happen?" He shook his head. "It's too late to worry, anyways." He turned to Raju. "Raju, quick, leave with Ma and hide behind the rock. Go, go."

"I'm not leaving without you," Vasu affirmed.

"Ma, please. You know I'm not leaving without Bali."

The rock was yards away and they were too late, he realised.

"Where's Maya?" Raju asked, panic growing within him.

"She's at the back of the enclosure. She'll come here with the men. They don't know she's with us... yet," Heera replied.

They could hear a clamour in the distance.

"It's time now," Heera said, setting his jaw. Putting his sack down, he looked inside to fetch two rocks he had picked earlier. "Ma, Raju, go hide inside that shelter." Heera pointed to the empty shelter closest to the rock. "And keep the torch with you. It's time we get help from the bees."

"I'm not going without you," Vasu said.

"Please, Ma, save yourselves from the bees. I

have the sap on me. There's no time. I have to go now."

He ran towards the tree with the hives. Closing one eye, he took aim and hurled the rock at the hives with all his might. It missed.

Bali's restless, guttural growls were sending tingles down his nerves. With trembling hands, he kissed the second one and flung it at the hives. It barely skimmed past them.

No! Heera ran back to where he had left his mother and Raju, to get his sack, his eyes scanning the ground on the way.

The surging men made an awful din, their panic-stricken voices growing stronger by the second. Heera was glad Raju and Vasu were hiding.

His eyes flitted past something on the ground and then settled on it; the bulky lock lying at the threshold of the shelter where Vasu had been imprisoned.

That'll do! Heera ran to fetch it, seizing his sack on the way.

"Who's that boy? Look," a man shouted, spotting Heera from a distance.

"He's back. The little rascal," another shouted. They ran towards him.

This time Heera was much closer to the tree. *Please forgive me, bees.* He took aim and threw the lock at the hive. The lock struck it with such force that a big chunk of the hive broke apart on impact with the solid chunk of metal, and fell, disturbing the bees in the hive below.

A swarm of hissing and fuming bees rose out of the tree like a dense cloud of black smoke.

It couldn't have been timed better. The men were right below it.

Caught off-guard by the buzzing assailants, the men ran helter-skelter. Some fell to the ground, shrieking in terror and pain from the stings.

Heera pulled the hacksaw out of his sack, and also the goat-skin bag with plant sap in it. Then he ran to Bali, blood pounding in his ears, bee stings stabbing his chest, arms and thighs. At least the sap kept the bees away from his face.

A flash of blue stood out amongst the men.

"Aaarh!" a scream escaped Maya's mouth. She was swatting at the bees that were stinging her legs.

"Maya! Maya!" Heera screamed.

Heera's voice was drowned in the disharmony of the yelling and groaning men, but Maya had seen him and she ran to him.

"Let's go to Bali," Heera told her when she was closer.

Maya ran to the enclosure, half-screaming, half-crying. When she got there, the sheer size of Bali and his panic shocked her.

The bees had reached Bali, even though in small

numbers. He tugged and tugged at the chain binding him. There was another one around his neck. He couldn't break free. His whimpers intensified. He flapped his ears to ward off the bees but there were some attacking his eyes. Cocking his head, he gave an earth-shattering trumpet.

Maya screwed her eyes shut and rammed her fingers in her ears to block out the sound threatening to burst her eardrums. She shuddered and stayed rooted to the ground. She wouldn't go near him, not without Heera.

Heera was almost at the enclosure when a powerful thrust in his lower back sent him crashing to the ground. The hacksaw and the goat-skin bag flew out of his hands. He flipped over onto his back and saw Mangal standing over him.

"You won't give up, will you, little rascal?" Mangal spat, whacking around madly at the bees, with his hands. He was badly stung on his face, which had broken out in great welts, making him look more villainous than ever. Nevertheless, he was determined to stop Heera.

Bali's terror was apparent. Heera knew it was critical for him to reach his dost and apply the plant-sap on his ears and eyes, or else it could be fatal for Bali.

Mangal stamped on Heera's leg above his ankle.

Heera winced in pain. His palms pressed against

the earth beneath him instinctively and he clutched at the fine soil. Grabbing a handful, he tossed it at Mangal's face.

Swearing, Mangal fell backwards, shrieking in rage and agony from the soil pricking his eyes, blinding him. Heera hauled himself up and kicked Mangal's stomach. Mangal bent forward in pain and blindly swiped a fist the size of a brick at Heera. Heera dodged it and jabbed his knee into Mangal's groin. Stunned by the impact, Mangal's mouth gaped open like a fish and he released a ragged wail, cramping forward in pain.

Maya ran to Heera. She picked up the hacksaw and the goat-skin bag. "Are you okay?" Her breath came in short gasps. She didn't wait for an answer. "Come with me, quick. Bali is petrified. You'll have to calm him down before I can go anywhere near him."

Most of the men around them had started to flee to save themselves from the bees. They didn't care about anything anymore. The smoke was rising in thick plumes. Heera and Maya were coughing.

Swatting at the bees, Heera entered Bali's pen with the bag of plant sap in his hands.

The elephant was swaying from side to side wildly, his tusks protruding formidably, his leg bloody from pulling against the chain.

"Bali! I'm here." Heera ran towards Bali and

stood in front of him, spreading his hands out as if wanting to embrace him. "Calm down." Bali's trumpet fell to a guttural rumble. Heera stepped forward. "It's only me, dost." Heera patted Bali's flank and he calmed down instantly. The taut chain at his leg clanged down on the ground, in peace.

Maya watched awe-struck.

Heera's heart wrenched at the sight of another chain around Bali's neck. However, it was imperative to attend to other things first.

"Let's get the bees off you," Heera said and took some sap on his palms. "Bend," he whispered gently. Bali bent his front leg and Heera climbed onto it. He applied some sap around Bali's ear and eye on one side. It began to deter the bees instantly. Bali relaxed and Heera dismounted his leg. He turned to Maya. "Come here, Maya. You can start to cut the chain while I apply some more sap to Bali. It'll take some time to get it around his ears."

Maya swallowed nervously. Stepping forward gingerly towards Bali and then around him, she bent low, watching the towering frame of the elephant above her and began to cut the chain at his leg with quivering hands.

"Don't worry, he won't hurt you," Heera encouraged her. "Slow, long strokes. You're doing well."

"He's bleeding," Maya said.

"I know. There's nothing we can do now. Keep going, we need to cut him free first." Heera continued smearing the plant sap on the other side of Bali's face. And Maya carried on hacking the chain but the varying tension in the chain due to Bali's movements made it difficult.

Heera noticed that the screaming outside the enclosure had died down. Most men had fled the area.

"Maya, you hold the chain taut. I'll cut. Will be faster," he said urgently.

Chewing the inside of his cheek, Heera began to hack at the chain on Bali's leg. He had cut more than halfway through it in minutes. Sweat dripped from his brow. Another minute and he had cut right through. His scalp prickled with relief.

"Now, the other chain. He didn't have one around his neck earlier."

Same as before, Maya held the chain taut while Heera started to cut through it. But this chain was twice as thick as the one on his leg and heavier too.

Less than halfway through the chain, Heera stopped. His nose tingled at a sharp, woody and familiar smell. *Cologne!*

Fear settled on him like a dark fog. Tension hung in the air, almost palpable.

He heard a gun being cocked, arrogant and crisp, confirming his doubts.

228

Heera flicked his eyes up and away from the chain.

Chapter Twenty-Seven

"Major Crook?" Heera gulped.

Crook stood at the entrance of the enclosure with two men, rigid, beside him.

The smoke had driven the bees away leaving hardly any to bother anyone, including the Major. Heera's grip on the handle of the hacksaw tightened until his knuckles went white.

Crook raised his rifle and pointed it at them. His reddened face twisted into a venomous stare and the veins in his neck pulsed.

"You've gone *too* far... *too* far to spoil my plans." Crook lifted his rifle to eye-level, then moved the barrel to point straight at Bali's head. His tone was so sharp that the words seemed to slash the air.

The language didn't make sense to Heera. But Crook's face, stiff with fury, and his action screamed his intention.

"NO," Heera ran in front of Bali. "NO. DON'T SHOOT!"

Crook threw his head back and laughed like a screeching seagull. "You think that'll change my mind, boy? I should have done this days ago."

"Do it, sahib." Mangal limped in behind Crook.

Crook aimed, ready to shoot.

Maya clutched her hand to her mouth on the verge of a scream.

BANG.

The gunshot reverberated through the space. Mind-numbing. And brutal.

BANG.

Another one sounded equally shameless as the one before.

Bali bellowed.

Time stopped.

The sense of loss was paralysing. Heera couldn't think. Nor could he scream.

His knees buckled below him, and he sank to the floor corpse-like. Immobile.

"AAAAAAARRRCHHH!"

The shouting shook Heera out of his daze.

"Get that – get that monkey off me," Crook yelled.

Heera dared to look up. Still shaking.

The Major was on the floor, covering his face

with his arms, while Basanti clawed at it. The rifle lay beside him.

The grating sound of metal above him caught Heera's attention and he looked up.

The two shots had hit the asbestos roof of the enclosure, leaving a gaping crack in the metal sheet, the edges of which scraped against each other as they moved in the wind.

Too much had happened too quickly. His mind struggled to understand. Probably, Basanti had attacked Crook, causing him to misfire. But that meant Raju was around too and most certainly with his mother.

Seeing Raju being attacked, Maya made a run towards him. One of the men who had stood beside Crook seized her, flinging his arm around her neck, pinning her body to his. Maya bit his hand above the wrist. The man yelled and let her go only to grab hold of her braid. He tugged ruthlessly.

Maya screamed.

Heera had darted in her direction, when the second man charged at him, striking him in his ribs. Heera fell to the ground. But the man had made a vital mistake not realising his proximity to Bali who was now cut free from the chain on his leg.

Bali raged ahead.

Immobilised by fear, the man gave a strangled cry. Bali thrashed the man's frame with his trunk, sending him flying metres away.

Reaching Maya, Heera swung the hacksaw at her captor. The blade caught the man's arm. With a scream, he backed off, watching the trickle of crimson on his arm.

Maya had a few seconds before her captor was out of his shock. Seizing the opportunity, she rammed her fingers into his eyes, adding to his agony.

"Ma," Heera cried, seeing his mother coming.

But Vasu ran straight to help Maya. She punched the man's nose so hard her knuckles hurt. He wavered and fell. Then Maya kicked his back.

Confident that the women had overpowered their assailant, Heera ran out of the enclosure.

He had heard a commotion outside.

Mangal had locked both of Raju's fists in one hand and held them tight. "Call that langoor of yours back and I'll let you go."

He twisted one of Raju's arms in a sudden jerk, up and behind his back.

Heera's heart surged with anger and, without stopping to think, he charged at Mangal.

Mangal clouted Heera's temple, knocking him backwards and filling his head with swirls and stars. But he had to let go of Raju. Raju darted at the torch that had fallen from his hands and thumped Mangal's bare back with it, branding him.

Mangal roared to face Raju; a man with lethal intentions.

Raju feinted with his right arm to distract him and then swung his left hand with the torch at Mangal's face. He missed. Instead, the blaze caught a chunky strand of Mangal's hair. And soon ballooned up across his head.

A look of sheer terror swept across Mangal's face. It was too much to take. Head on fire, he ran shrieking.

Raju blew out his cheeks and closed his eyes.

The fire had spread to the shelter closest to the enclosure. The flames licked the branches of the tree that hung above the shelter holding the bee hives.

BANG.

Bali curled his trunk upwards and screeched.

Heera doubled over with cramps at the sound of the gunshot. It was as if a lead ball had dropped in his stomach and was blocking his gut.

His eyes darted to where the Major had fallen.

He wasn't there. Neither was his rifle.

Instead, Basanti's limp body lay there, in a pool of blood.

Chapter Twenty-Eight

"NOOOO!" Raju cried.

Heera's jaw dropped open in horror. His heart contorted with agony.

Bali's trumpeting dipped to a dull whimper.

Raju dashed towards the enclosure and fell to his knees beside Basanti. "Oh, Basanti!" The gripping pain in his heart was reflected in his haunted expression. He reached out to the macaque's body with quivering hands.

Thank you. Heera sat down next to Raju and bowed his head down in gratitude and respect. He would remain indebted to the macaque as long as he lived. She had saved Bali by causing the Major to misfire.

"Are we done paying respects then?" Crook scorned, stepping in from the side of the enclosure, nudging Maya and Vasu ahead with the barrel of his rifle. Maya grabbed the fabric of her skirt so tight that her knuckles went white. "You'll have plenty more to pay respects to, I guarantee that." Crook's steely grey eyes bore holes into Heera.

"You wanted to kill Bali and now you've killed my Basanti." Raju's nostrils flared, every word seething with fury. "You're a killer. A brute. A maniac."

Crook didn't understand a word, but felt the anger. "Whatever gibberish nonsense that was, I don't care. I'm having this elephant and *none* of you can stop me. *Not today. Not tomorrow.* NEVER!" Spittle flew from his mouth. He shoved the women ahead with his weapon. "I'm not going to shoot you all! No, no, no. I'm not stupid now, am I?" Crook advanced with Maya and Vasu ahead of him, towards Heera and Raju. His face was sweaty like everyone else from the heat and also bloody from Basanti's bite marks. "Up," he gestured with his finger. "Up, you two and walk, or else," he pointed at Bali's head with the rifle. "I'll crack his brains open."

Standing up, Heera threw his arms up in surrender and so did Raju with a scowl on his face and tears in his eyes.

"Good!" Crook said. "So, what was I saying? Ah! Yes, that I won't be shooting you. Instead, I'll be *roasting* you all. We'll make it all look like an accident. NOW MARCH." Crook thrust his rifle into Vasu's back, and she stumbled forward. Maya was trying hard not to cry.

Heera glanced at Bali who was yanking at the chain at his neck to break free.

The boys continued to retreat; the Major continued advancing.

The burning shelter was very close behind them. The heat was now unbearable and the smoke thick. The branches of the tree – with the hives on it – crackled in the flames, firing out sparks.

Even though his words didn't make sense, the Major's intentions were as clear as day.

Maya's mouth twisted into a scream that never came, looking at the blazing inferno in front of her. Vasu's eyes glazed in horror.

Bali's trumpets, the rattling and clanking of the metal chains continued, although Bali was now out of Heera's line of sight.

"Saarrry, sahib. Saary!" Heera held his ears and begged for forgiveness with one of the few words he knew in the English language – '*sorry*'. "No, sahib. No." Heera fell to his knees and bent to touch his forehead to the ground.

"Get up, you clumsy rascal," Crook spat.

"No, sahib," Heera held on to the Major's shoe. "No. No," he grovelled. "We'll serve you our whole life. Please let us go, sahib."

Vasu looked on in a mixture of bewilderment and

anguish.

"What *nonsense* is this?" The Major shook his foot, but Heera didn't let go. With one big shove, he kicked Heera away.

"Heera!" Vasu wept.

Then the ground vibrated. Heera's ears were almost touching the earth and he could sense the tremors ripple through it. Anticipation and joy and fear made him shudder.

He raised his head. An enormous, grey-black outline – hazy at first and camouflaged in the smoke surrounding it – floated towards them. Two massive, white tusks protruded through the curtain of smoke.

BALI! A sizzle of hope ran through Heera. He had timed it right.

Heera knew he had cut halfway through the chain on Bali's neck, but the Major didn't. There was no way out of there, unless he could buy Bali more time to get himself free. And that was what the grovelling was all about.

Raju's eyes widened. His jaw dropped open.

Registering the look in Raju's eyes, Crook turned to find himself barely a foot away from a fuming elephant. Air left his lungs and he faltered backwards towards Raju.

Heera leaped up with alacrity and grabbed Crook's rifle from his hands, now limp with shock.

"N-no. B-back off," Crook stammered, his

tongue thick and heavy in his mouth.

Heera could read Bali's eyes; unforgiving and unyielding.

Pushing Raju, Maya, and his mother out of the way, he himself cleared the path for Bali.

That left Crook standing between the inferno and the raging animal in front of him, too petrified to scream.

With one giant whisk of his trunk, Bali swept Crook off the ground as if picking up a doll. Holding the Major above his head, dangling from his trunk like a lifeless puppet, Bali hurled him into the heart of the burning shed.

Chapter Twenty-Nine

A week later, the trio sat on the riverbank, dangling their legs into the cool water.

"Exactly a week ago," Raju said, stroking Basanti's lead in his hand. His eyes welled up.

"She was a heroine," Heera said, empathising with Raju's pain.

"Yes, she was," Maya asserted. "It was her who stopped the Major from shooting Bali. Did you teach her to attack like that?"

"Yes," Raju, said wiping his eyes. "She was bright and a quick learner. But opening locks she already knew," he smiled. "Long before I found her, she used to perform on the streets. But she was ill-treated by her owner. He had left her to die after she was injured in a macaque fight."

"That's awful," Maya replied.

Bali, who was in the river, sprayed a jet of water

on them making them squeal.

Heera caught sight of the tattoo on Raju's arm when he lifted it to cover his face.

"Raju, can I ask you something?"

"You already have." Maya laughed.

"Go on," Raju replied.

"Where did you get that tattoo – the one on the inside of your arm?"

"Oh, that!" Raju said lifting his arm. "I don't know. Baba said I always had it. Why? Why do you ask?"

"Nothing."

"Oh, come on. There has to be something. That's why you asked," Maya said.

Heera showed them his tattoo.

Maya gasped.

"Isn't this – show me." Maya compared Raju's tattoo to it. "They're exactly the same! What a brilliant coincidence!"

Heera half-smiled, unconvinced.

"Perhaps you belonged to a tribe. But you wouldn't know, would you?"

Raju shook his head. "No. Baba adopted me when I was a baby."

"A tribe?" Maya asked.

"Members of a family in our tribe get identical tattoos."

"You belong to a tribe?" Raju queried.

"I do. But Ma was banished for marrying outside it. My father didn't belong to her tribe."

"Love and sacrifice!" Maya said dreamily.

Raju harrumphed to bring her back, and Maya instantly blushed.

"You two could be cousins," she said, quickly hiding her awkwardness.

Raju's bright eyes danced with excitement. "There's not much I know about where I come from. Although, there's something really precious I have."

The next day, Raju met Heera under a mango tree near Heera's hut. The honied fragrance of the ripening fruit was irresistible.

After feasting on it for lunch, Raju pulled out a silver, circular piece of metal from his pocket.

Heera was still sucking at the mango stone, trying to extract every drop of pulpy sweetness.

"This is what I was talking about," Raju said. "My only precious possession."

The mango stone slipped from Heera's hands and landed on the soil.

"Show me." Heera took it and stared. He was holding an exact copy of the silver anklet he had seen in his dreams and in his mother's trunk. It had the same letters inscribed on it, that he had memorised as patterns seen on his anklet. "Where did you get that?" Heera asked, his muscles rigid.

"I didn't find it. Baba said I was wearing it on my ankle when he found me."

"It's an anklet!" Heera muttered.

"Yes! Doesn't fit me anymore. Obviously must have, when I was younger."

"Where did Baba find you?"

"At the riverbank afloat in a basket."

"What?!"

"Yes. He had been washing his clothes at the riverbank. This was years ago, of course."

Heera darted to his hut.

"Hey! Give it back," Raju cried and dashed after Heera.

Vasu was busy stirring a pot full of curry.

"Hungry already?" She smiled.

Unheeding, Heera ran to pull the trunk out.

Raju stopped at the door.

Rummaging through the box, Heera recklessly pulled the vermillion saree out and shook it wildly.

"What are you doing?" Vasu exclaimed. "What is the matter with you?"

The anklet clanked to the floor and rolled towards Vasu. Heera's haunted eyes followed it.

Heera held out the anklet he had taken from Raju.

"What's that?" Vasu snatched it off him and looked closely. Her jaw quivered and her eyes rushed from the anklet in her hand to the one on the floor.

"I've always asked you, Ma. About the anklet. About my dreams." Heera's voice was as taut as a bowstring. "Can you tell me the *truth* for once?"

As if in a trance, words floated out of Vasu's mouth in a whisper, "Where did you find it?"

"It's… mine," Raju said cautiously.

"Tell her what you told me, Raju" Heera said.

"What's going on?" Raju was puzzled.

Heera picked up the anklet on the floor and held it to Raju's face. "This one is mine."

Raju peered at it. "This is exactly…" He looked at his anklet in Vasu's hands. "…identical to mine. How come?"

"Ask my mother. She should know." Heera shot Vasu a gruff look. "Raju isn't Rajveer's son, Ma. Rajveer found him wearing the anklet as a baby." Heera turned to Raju. "Tell her, Raju."

Raju told Vasu how his Baba had found him floating in a basket in a river in a neighbouring town.

Vasu listened carefully. And her chin started to tremble.

"Show her your tattoo," Heera demanded.

"My tattoo?!" Raju exposed his inner arm hesitantly. "Are we related, like Maya said?" he asked.

Seeing the tattoo, Vasu slumped on the floor with a moan, like a puppet with its strings cut.

Heera ran to Vasu's side. "Ma, are you okay?"

Vasu nodded. Tears scalded her cheeks. She was crying and laughing both at the same time.

"Thank you. Thank you. Thank you!" Vasu cried, clasping her palms together and bending forward. "Thank you, Shiva!"

Befuddled, Raju looked at Heera and back at Vasu.

"Come here... son," Vasu beckoned Raju. Raju tentatively stepped forward. "Sit." Raju squatted next to her, uncertain and restive. She peered at his face with a softness he hadn't known before. The similarity was undeniable. "You have my eyes." Vasu's voice trailed off into a low sigh and she squeezed Raju's arm.

The truth hit Heera like a rock. The familiarity of Raju's face and eyes had mystified him right from the start, ever since he met Raju in the bazaar for the very first time.

"Is he my—" Heera stopped mid-sentence, choking on his own words.

Vasu nodded, knowing what Heera had meant to ask. "Forgive me, child. I've lied to you all along." She tapped Heera's cheek and looked away into a distant place only she could go. "Sometimes, life forces you to make difficult choices. Once, long ago, a mother had to make such a choice. She had to choose between her two children, because there was

245

only one she could save. And she did. Not preferring one child over the other, just doing what she could... What she thought was right... She had to, because she couldn't have saved both. That day was the single most excruciatingly painful day of her life." Vasu stifled a sob. Her eyes floated to Raju. "The day she had to let go of her baby after the basket carrying him accidentally slipped and fell into the river while the other child was on the banks." Her voice trembled. "The woman was torn between the two. Her heart ripped apart watching her baby slip away. She ran with the other child in her arms following him along the banks, but couldn't carry on. Neither could she abandon the child in her arms and jump into the water, as much as she wished to." Vasu sniffled and wiped her nose with her saree. "But not one day went by when she didn't think of her other baby. Not one day passed by when she didn't blame herself for not being able to save them both. And not one day passed by when she didn't ask God to keep her lost child alive and safe and for him to forgive her." Vasu brought her palms together in front of her and bent her head, bursting into tears. "Raju, forgive your mother. I failed you."

Trembling, Raju threw his arms around Vasu and forced himself to say the word out aloud. "Ma." Its warmth resonated in his spirit.

"I have a brother!" Heera heard himself say.

"Younger brother," Vasu corrected him, sniffling. "He used to cry a lot, especially after he had that tattoo."

As if Heera had waited for her to say this all his life, a sizzle of faint memories arose. He recognised they had been prodding him in his dreams.

Heera threw his arms around the two, joy swelling inside him; he could have burst.

Far away, somewhere in the forest, a familiar trumpet sounded, and Heera knew he would now live as rich as his name.

Acknowledgements

When I started writing this book, I had nothing more than an image of a young boy running through an Indian tropical forest in a dhoti. All I knew then was that I wanted to write about India and share a glimpse of my childhood which was spent amongst dearest family, friends, and nature (and that was absolutely not during the British Raj but much, much later, in case you are wondering). In time, the story revealed itself spontaneously, word after word, page after page, even on days when I had no idea what I was going to write.

I would like to thank the entire team at SRL Publishing, especially Stuart Debar for publishing *The Elephant Heist* and for helping me realise my dream of seeing it in print. Thank you for your patience in answering the millions of questions I have asked and for pretending they were all sensible and justified. Thanks to the very talented Holly Dunn for the brilliant and magical cover design. You brought my vision to life, impeccably. It is absolutely stunning. Thanks to CJ Harter for her editorial inputs and suggestions. It was great to have someone experienced look at the novel with a fresh pair of eyes.

It took a lot of perseverance and discipline on my part to write this book, particularly the final quarter which was written during the pandemic and lockdown. However, no man is an island and so is no woman. A lot of unseen hands have contributed to this book and enhanced my efforts whilst writing it.

Thanks to my husband – my rock – for bearing with

me on my not-so-good-writing days that, quite frequently, turned into not-so-good-cooking and even not-so-good-mood days. And for being there unconditionally (I am trying hard not to sound soppy here) and equally not being there when I needed some peace and quiet.

Bear hugs to my children for their suggestions, feedback, and involvement in my writing journey. To Siya who can talk for eons but instead spent eons reading my manuscript for the millionth time. And to Pratham for taking time off *FIFA* to give his mature and constructive criticism. Thank you, my darlings, for always believing in me and cheering me on.

Big thanks to my parents. I couldn't have done it without your genetic material. I have to admit that you were right, Papa, when you told me I would write fiction one day. And Ma, I would still be hesitating to hit *send* on my submission emails without your morale boosters. Thanks for keeping my spirits high when I thought I was not good enough and that nobody would ever publish anything I wrote.

A big shout out to the judging panel of the SCBWI BAME Scholarship Awards and Gemma Cooper, in particular, for giving me the honorary mention for this novel in 2019. That propelled me on to complete it.

I cannot end without a heartfelt thanks to Barry Cunningham and the team at Chicken House Publishing for longlisting this novel in the *Times Chicken House Competition 2020*. It was a game changer and made me believe in myself more than ever. Kesia Lupo, thank you for your encouragement, feedback, and review on this book.

SRL Publishing don't just publish books, we also do our best in keeping this world sustainable. In the UK alone, over 77 million books are destroyed each year, unsold and unread, due to overproduction and bigger profit margins.

Our business model is inherently sustainable by only printing what we sell. While this means our cost price is much higher, it means we have minimum waste and zero returns. We made a public promise in 2020 to never overprint our books for the sake of profit.

We give back to our planet by calculating the number of trees used for our products so we can then replace them. We also calculate our carbon emissions and support projects which reduce CO_2. These same projects also support the United Nations Sustainable Development Goals.

The way we operate means we knowingly waive our profit margins for the sake of the environment. Every book sold via the SRL website plants at least one tree.

To find out more, please visit
www.srlpublishing.co.uk/responsibility

Lightning Source UK Ltd.
Milton Keynes UK
UKHW042303230223
417554UK00001B/10